The Milford Farm And Other Christmas Stories

J. Mark Van Valin

To our church families
spread across the miles and years,
with whom Linda and I and our children
shared the candlelight and the mystery on
many a Christmas Eve.

May our Lord keep us until the day we are
reunited together with Him in Glory.

Acknowledgements

I am grateful to the loving church families I have served over the years: The Lighthouse Free Methodist Church in St. Louis, MO (my first assignment), the West Morris Street Free Methodist Church in Indianapolis, IN (where our three children grew up) and the Spring Arbor Free Methodist Church in south central Michigan.

These stories were tried out on those people, my people – who worshiped and served, celebrated and grieved, and loved and laughed with us. The stories were shaped in part by the life our family shared with those congregations.

I want to thank my friend Dan Runyon, Professor at Spring Arbor University, who has years of writing and publishing experience. From time to time, as his pastor, he would tell me I should put some things in print. I am thankful for his counsel and encouragement.

I am thankful for my wife, Linda and our wonderful children, Kristin, John David, and Andrew. The kids are now grown and married with children of their own. My storytelling skills were honed years ago on them. After tucking them in at night, I would often lie down on the hallway floor between their bedrooms and come up with stories on the spot. I would tell stories of my childhood, the crime-stopping adventures of Moms Mabley (borrowing the name but little else from the real-life comedian), and a whole series on the Mysterious Fog.

The stories had their effect, I suppose, because more often than not, I would fall asleep before they did, drifting off in mid-sentence.

I now get to do it all again with our seven grandchildren – Abigail, Elsie, Liam, Madeleine, Micah, Minta Rose (born in November), and now little Colette, born just today.

God is so good.

MVV
December 20, 2019

Contents

Introduction
The Story Behind the Stories

Out of the entire church year, the Christmas Eve service has always been my favorite. The whole church community, out of town guests, the carols, the anticipation, the garland, the candlelight, and the threat of snow - all make for a magical evening.

Having served as a pastor for over thirty-six years, I cannot remember preaching a sermon on Christmas Eve. I usually have told a story. Over time, some have been forgotten. Some were not worth telling again. Some have been kept alive to be retold, but always with a bit of extra steak sauce.

The following pages contain nine of those stories. They are arranged chronologically according to the year I remember introducing them. The gaps in some years means that a story was told that has been forgotten, or an old story was brought out of moth balls and told again. *Christmas on the Milford Farm* has been repeated numerous times over the years.

All the stories are fictional, except for *The Stupid Gift.* That really happened. Just ask my brother. Apart from the Biblical characters, all the figures are also fictional, except for Grandma Campbell in *Mother Mary.* That character is based on the real-life Gladys "Grandma" Smith, who served in our children's department at the Free Methodist church in Dearborn, MI when I was a boy. Children who attended there in the 1950's and 1960's would know her. Her hugs were memorable.

As far as art goes, these short stories don't qualify as serious literature. They were written for and told to kids and adults alike. They cannot be categorized as being exclusively for either children or adults. I do hope readers of every age will glean something from them.

Crafting stories around the theme of Christmas has always been a delight. The incarnation of the Creator of the universe, crossing the great chasm to redeem a broken world, is the defining narrative of history. There is no limit to the beauty, the drama, and the irony of it all - donkeys and sheep, angels and shepherds, wise men and gifts, mysterious signs in the heavens, evil villains, conspiracy and danger, the complicated love story of Joseph and Mary - all centered around a baby in a manger.

In his wisdom, or cosmic sense of humor, God saw fit to package Jesus' coming in a way that befuddles theologians while delighting children. I wonder if He will do the same when He comes again.

The name of Jesus appears rarely in these pages, yet he is everywhere. I think it was C.S. Lewis who compared Jesus to the sun. We cannot stare directly at him for long, yet by his light we see everything else more clearly.

I have simply tried to tell the stories behind the Story, in hopes that the powerful drama of Jesus' birth might grow as large in the imagination as it really is.

We know that this is impossible. Our finite hearts and heads simply do not have the capacity to fully contain the thing. Yet we must try. Where prose fails, music, art, and poetry have helped us along.

All I have to offer here, however, are words. In light of the wonders of Christ's birth, my best attempts with words might come off (borrowing a phrase from Garrison Keillor) as a "handful of dried peas rattling around in a can".

But all is not lost. It is simply a humbling reminder that the glory of Christmas is infinitely greater than any person can describe it.

In any case, I hope you enjoy reading these stories as much as I had writing them.

MVV

Christmas on the Milford Farm
Christmas Eve 1992

It has been a cold week at the Milford farm. Last Thursday was the coldest of all, and also the shortest. Old farmer Milford spent the entire day working in the barn, cleaning out stalls, winterizing the tractor, and putting down fresh straw. He fed all the animals, cleaned out the trough, filled it with fresh water, then placed a heating element in it to keep it from freezing.

He finished just as the sun was going down. He gave everything a final look, turned out the lights and headed back to the house. The barn went dark, except for a faint light leaking through the slats in the siding, coming from the yellow bulb hanging outside over the door.

The animals were all parked in their stalls. They weren't tired. After all, it was still early.

There were Orville and Wilbur, the work horses. They were brothers, of course. Then there were B-e-e-e-n-n-n and B-o-o-o-n-n-i-e, the lambs. There was Thumbelina the cow, and Henrietta and Marletta the chickens. Up in the rafters was Zoe the mourning dove. Then there was Mort, the pig.

Mort was the spokesman of the group.

They all lay there, whispering to each other in the dark, telling jokes. Someone would make a funny noise, and they'd all giggle.

One of them called over to Mort who was lounging in the far stall on the left. "Mort, tell us a story."

"Oh, I don't know if I can remember any," he grunted.

"Yes, you do. We know you do. Tell us a story."

Then Zoe called down from the rafter, "Tell us the story of the Boy Child!"

Mort hesitated. "Oh, it's been a long time since I've told that one. I don't know if I can remember it all."

"I-I-I-I reme-e-e-mber you telling i-i-i-i-t," said Bonnie. "Yes!" another one blurted out. "Tell us the story about the Boy Child." They all chimed in. "Yes, Mort. Tell us, please!"

Mort gave a low grunt, then surrendered. "Well, O.K."

He waddled out of his stall and ambled towards the center of the barn where the old John Deere was parked.

He climbed up on the tractor, plopped down on the seat, spun around backwards and leaned back against the steering wheel, crossing one leg over the other. You know, the way pigs do.

He closed his eyes, lifted his head, and began.

"It was a long time ago, and far, far away. It happened on a farm much like this one, and on a night just about as cold as this one.

"But it was a perilous time for residents like us."

(Now, I need to explain to you, the reader, that this is how domestic farm animals refer to themselves. They call themselves "residents." No one can really explain why. It is just the way it has always been.)

Mort continued.

"It was a time where the upright ones . . ."

(Allow me to say one other thing. "Upright ones" is the name that domestic animals have for us humans. Again, no one knows how or where it originated. Though one might, perhaps, see the logic behind the label, the irony of it is hard to miss.)

"It was a time when the upright ones had a frightful

15

practice. Back in those days, whenever one of them would do something wrong, or fail to do the right thing – which was quite often - they could be relieved of their guilt by carrying out the punishment on one of us residents. They would take it out on us."

The animals groaned.

"Residents would be at home, minding their own business, when suddenly an upright one would burst in, grab one of the them, and you'd never see them again. It was life for life."

"Did they do this all the time?" Zoe asked Mort.

"Yes, but more often at certain times of the year."

"Did they take their sins out on everyone?" clucked Henrietta.

"Pretty much," Mort said.

"Did they take cows?" asked Thumbelina.

"Oh yes, they took cows, lots of cows."

"How about doves?" asked Zoe.

"Certainly, doves, of course."

"W-h-h-h-at about la-a-a-mbs?" cried Bonnie.

"Oh, lambs most of all," said Mort. "They especially loved lambs."

The animals shuddered at the horror of it. "What about pigs?" they said. Mort rubbed his chin and thought for a second.

"Come to think of it, pigs were exempt."

They all squinted at him, but they knew it must be true.

"The days were fraught with danger, and never more than on this particular day. By decree, the upright ones had to travel, each to their birthplace, and the nearby town was filled with them. Thousands had come from every direction. And as you might guess, whenever crowds of upright ones gathered, unfortunate things happened. More of them needed to cleanse themselves of their guilt.

"All through the day they came, the door would fly open and out would go a cow or a dove or a lamb. The residents trembled in the dark corners of the barn in terror, hoping against hope to survive.

"It was a frightful day, but as the sun was going down, the residents began to grow hopeful, feeling maybe they could finally let down their guard. The upright ones usually didn't come after dark.

"Evening came and the residents, with great relief, began to relax. The night grew late, and one by one, they came out from the shadows and into the open.

"But just when they felt that they were out of danger, they were startled by the sound of voices outside the door. They heard the shuffling of feet. Their hearts stopped. The residents scurried to the back corners of the barn and held their breath. The latch turned, the door creaked open, and the cold wind poured in. The residents were paralyzed with fear.

"In the darkness they could make out a tall figure, an upright one, backing slowly in through the door and into the barn. He was pulling on a rope. His head was down and he looked tired. On the other end of the rope was a donkey. On the donkey sat a young woman. She was slumped forward, covered in a blanket. Her head rested on the animal's neck. She looked sick. Though the night was cold, she was soaked with perspiration. Her eyes were closed and her face was taut with pain. She clutched the mane of the donkey. She cried out in distress, then she went silent. She cried out again about two minutes later, and silent again. This went on for some time.

"The man pulled the donkey into the barn and closed the door behind him. He didn't seem interested in the residents. Their curiosity grew. They crept closer, out from the shadows and into what light there was to get a better look.

"The man lit a lantern, found an empty stall, arranged the straw into a soft bed, then laid a blanket on the straw. He turned towards the girl, lifted her off the donkey, and gently laid her on the blanket. She moaned as the pain came on her in waves. 'She must be dying,' the residents thought.

"The man moved quickly. He drew some water from the trough, arranged what few blankets he had, then removed his undergarment and starting tearing it into strips of cloth.

"The residents moved closer.

"He leaned over the young girl and spoke tenderly to her, gently caressing her back and neck. She took a deep breath, let out one last forceful cry and then fell silent.

"She must be dead," they all concluded.

"But after a moment, they heard a muffled whimper, then a loud cry. It didn't come from the girl. It was a baby. The girl had been in labor the whole time. She had given birth to a baby!

"The residents quietly crept closer and surrounded the stall. They could see the steam rise off of the child's wrinkled, pink body. It was a boy child. The man cut the umbilical cord, cleaned the baby as best he could, wrapped him in the strips of cloth and then laid him in the girl's arms.

"He tended to both her and the child until they were quiet, then he collapsed next to them on the mound of straw. He tucked his legs up to his chest and rested his head on his knees. After several minutes, he began to sing. He lifted his eyes and quietly sang a song about a lamb. When he was done, he dropped his head in exhaustion.

Then he wept. And then he slept.

And the residents kept watch.

"In the early hours, before morning, the door flew open and several upright ones burst in. The residents scattered, but the visitors had not come for them. They were there to see the baby. They were shepherds. They stayed no more than a minute or two, spoke briefly to the man, then left laughing with wonder and joy as they headed back out into the night.

"Before the sun came up, the man, the young girl, and the Boy Child were gone."

Mort stopped, and the barn was quiet. Someone finally asked, "Then what happened?"

"Well," Mort said. "The Boy Child grew, and he went about the entire country, teaching the upright ones. He told them stories about the Maker and he told them what was to come. He did amazing things. He healed the sick, raised the dead, and delivered many from the evil one. He went about doing good.

"Most of the upright ones loved him. They followed him wherever he went. There were, however, powerful upright ones in the land who feared him. They were threatened by his wisdom, authority, and power. The Boy Child was turning the world right side up, and they were afraid they would lose their place.

"They plotted to kill him, and eventually they succeeded. They arrested him and accused him of this crime and that, but he did nothing wrong. In fact, he was the only upright one who got everything right. He was altogether good. And they killed him."

"Ohhh," the animals groaned. "That is a sad story."

"But no," Mort stopped them. "That's not the end of it. Yes, the powerful upright ones killed the Boy Child, but they could not have touched him if he had not let them.

"But he did let them. His followers buried him, but three days later, the Boy Child came up out of the grave. He was alive! He was seen by many who followed him, and they went out from there to tell the whole world about the risen Boy Child.

"It is said that he lives today and is going to return someday to set everything right."

"Everything?" they asked.

"Yes. Everything, and us too."

The animals sighed wistfully. "Ohhh!"

"But there is something more." Mort pondered. "It is the strangest and most wonderful thing."

"You see, ever since the upright ones killed the Boy Child, they stopped laying their sins on us." He paused, and then his voice took on a hushed reverence the others had rarely heard out of him.

"It was as if he died for us."

The animals were greatly moved by this.

Thumbelina eventually spoke up, "Did that really happen? Is it true?"

Mort answered, "Every word."

None of them moved. There was not a sound in the barn except for the wind whistling through the slats in the siding.

Then, from up in the rafters, Zoe, the mourning dove, began to sing. It was a simple, sweet melody, wistful with longing and hope. They all listened, their heads nodding as something about the melody resonated deep within them.

Then one by one, they all joined in. None of them had sung it before, but they all knew it. It was a Song of Creation.

Orville and Wilbur laid down the bass line with their deep baritone voices.

B-e-n-n-n and B-o-n-n-n-n-n-i-e lamb chimed in with their lovely vibrato.

Thumbelina lowed in gentle legato tones.

Henrietta and Marletta kept time with their clucking.

And Mort joined in with his low monotone.

The all sang. It was lovely – the ancient Song of Creation, the song about the Boy Child.

I wasn't there. I wish I had been there, but I wasn't there to hear it, the Song of Creation. I hope, however, to hear it someday, when the Boy Child comes again, when all creation will see Him together, and everything will be made new.

And on that day, the upright ones, the living creatures, the rocks and trees, the mountains, the distant galaxies – will joyfully sing together to the glory of the Boy Child.

The Donkey King
Christmas Day, 2005

Sol was young and ambitious, just out of business school. He talked his father-in-law out of a small loan to start his own company. The idea was a new and used donkey enterprise. His advertising pitch was "Hee-haw what a deal!" He had a sign and some stationary made and crowned himself "The Donkey King."

He made his first payment on an abandoned property south of Jerusalem, along an old and lightly traveled road that passed by the eastern edge of Bethlehem. He rented a used tent and set up his donkey lot. Not one to be afraid of hard work, he advertised his hours as sun-up to sundown. The tent was a three-flapper. He would run a three--bay full-service garage, a one stop operation. He would take trade-ins too.

Everything was going according to schedule. He had opening day circled on his calendar. To avoid inventory, he wanted to wait until after tax season. He had bartered for a few select used animals. He made a deal with a nearby farmer who would breed his animals on contract to be paid on delivery. He had lithe, nimble donkeys for climbing. He had broad half ton models for large loads.

He had a smart one for transportation and a couple dumb ones for pulling. He was hoping for a deluxe model for breeding and some mules for heavy labor. That would have to come in time.

He worked all week getting everything ready. The sign was out and his wife had put up colored streamers which flapped invitingly in the light breeze. He bought a load of pomegranates to use as giveaways for anyone who would test drive a new model.

The special day finally arrived. Sol lit some torches in front of the entrance and out along the road. He hired his cousin Sammy to play his pipe and do a few card tricks for entertainment.

"Everybody in your places!" he cried as the sun was coming up. "Everyone" was just Sol, his wife, and Sammy. Sol pulled back the tent flaps, stood at the entrance, and waited.

And he waited.

Morning gave way to afternoon. The bell on the tent cord hadn't rung one time. Sol pretended to be busy. About 3:00 Sammy went home. "I'll pay you tomorrow," Sol said earnestly.

Soon the sun was going down. Sol's wife had gone home too. She said she had to wash her hair.

Sol hadn't seen a soul on the road all day, let alone anyone who would stop in. "Oh well, it's only one day," he sighed. "These things take time. The word will get out . . . some way."

"Who are you kidding?" the practical side of his brain shouted. "Your location is wrong. Traffic has all swung to the north. The growing edge of town is up towards Bethany."

"You're as dumb as a mule," Sol said partly to himself and also to an old mount gnawing on a rope. The animal just looked away.

Sol counted the money in the till one more time. It was well past the twelfth hour and the sun had already set. He thought he'd close up and try again tomorrow. No use staying open for customers who didn't even know they were customers yet.

He put the seed money in the box and hid it under a board that covered a hole he'd dug in the sand. He blew out the remaining torch, and was just about to close the last tent flap and take down the sign, when he heard someone coming.

A young man was standing outside the tent with a young girl straddling a haggard-looking mule. "Peace be to you," nodded the man wearily. The girl gave a faint smile. Even in the dark, Sol could tell the mule had a lot of miles on it. A baby in the girl's arms whimpered. Draped over the side of the animal were a few small bags.

"I saw your sign and was hoping you might still be open. I know it's late, but we need a fresh mount for my wife and baby. We have some distance to go. Can you help us?"

Sol's heart raced. He regained his composure, pasted on his best smile, then chirped in his cheeriest sales voice, "What is it that I can interest you in?"

The man answered wearily. "We are heading south a good distance. We cannot stop for the night. We have to keep going. We just came from Nazareth for the registration. We were planning on going back north, but our plans have changed. Our mount is spent. We were going to continue in hopes that she would hold out, but the risk of being stranded in the wilderness at night is too great, and then we saw the sign. We cannot go back Jerusalem way. We have to travel the foothills at night and circle to the east, and then south."

"Where are you heading in such a hurry?"

The man hesitated, looked at the girl, who nodded to him. "Egypt," he volunteered.

"Egypt!" Sol thought. "That's a long way off. They must be in trouble." His better judgment told him not to ask.

The man continued, "I know this all seems out of the ordinary. Even if we had time to explain, you could make no more sense of it than we can. I only know we must hurry on if we can."

Sol studied the man. He was young and he seemed conscientious enough. He steadied the young girl on the donkey. She had to be no more than sixteen or seventeen. The baby was a newborn, only a couple weeks at best.

What were they doing way out here? The man kept glancing nervously over his shoulder, scanning the horizon to the north. "Who must be after them?" Sol thought. They seemed innocent enough, even sincere, but he learned long ago that it was the harmless-looking ones you had to worry about the most. Anyway, whatever danger they were in was none of his concern.

"I have a slightly used mule that was in service in the military. It is sure-footed and will travel the foothills quite well. Could I interest you in it?"

"That would be very good," said the young man.

"I think I can give you a good deal on it."

The young man's countenance fell. He looked down at the ground. "There is only a small problem, Sir." He took in a breath and sighed. "I have very little I can pay you."

Sol felt like someone had just punched him in the stomach. He rolled his eyes and then the man spoke again, with a halting voice.

"We packed only enough to come to Bethlehem and then return home after a short stay. Now we have barely enough to make it to our destination, let alone to survive once we get there.

"Well now," Sol said as he straightened up and put his hands on his hips. "This is another matter altogether. Where is it you said you were going?

"Egypt," the young man said, "although I cannot tell you exactly where. That is yet to be determined."

"And where did you say you were from?"

"Nazareth." The man cleared his throat and looked away.

Sol crossed his arms and nodded his head, "I should have known. Credit is not much good there, you know."

"I know," said the young man. He turned towards the girl and placed his hand on hers. "And what is more, I cannot tell you if or when we will ever be back this way. Only the Lord knows. We can only do as he says. He has told us to go."

Sol looked down, pulled at his beard and kicked the dirt a bit. They looked so pitiful. He was never one to suffer fools. He had even less patience for religious nuts. What a first day of business! Only one customer and a non-paying one at that. What did they take him for? Why waste time even talking to these two? Yet, in a rare moment, for him at least, he felt a twinge of compassion.

"Do you have anything at all you can use as payment? Collateral? Beyond this old trade-in?

The couple looked at each other. The girl reached into the satchel. "We have three small gifts that were given to the baby." The man took the bag and pulled out a small amount of gold, a jar of incense, and a vial of expensive myrrh, a burial ointment. "This is all we have to live on, but we have to get there first. What is your price?"

Sol shook his head. He concluded that criminals

would have better sense than these two, so they can't be criminals. If they were dishonest, they would have come up with a better story than this. Whoever was after them must have a reason, or they must be paranoid. The couple's story was farfetched enough that they just might be telling the truth.

"Do you have family in Nazareth?"

"Oh yes. They are expecting us back within the month, but they do not know. . they must not know we are going away."

Sol couldn't hold his curiosity any longer. "Excuse me for asking. Just why do you have to leave the country? Have you committed a crime?"

"Not that we can tell," said the young man. "It is because of the child. We have been warned the king is searching for him. He wants to take his life."

"Herod?"

"Yes sir."

"Who is this child?" he asked. "Are you his parents?"

"Yes. . . Well. . . No. . .I mean, yes. She is his mother. And I am . . . I am entrusted to care for him. The Lord has told me this is what I am to do."

Sol was more confused than ever. "So, the Lord has need of a donkey?"

The young man smiled, "I suppose so, more than you know. The Lord most certainly has need of it."

Sol thought he was losing it right there. He was never warned of this kind of thing in business school. He could deal with shysters and cons, foot-draggers and hoof-kickers, but this . . . He was dumbfounded. Good thing his wife wasn't here. She'd lock him up for sure.

He exhaled a deep sigh and then started untying the army mule, muttering to himself the whole time. "The Lord owns the cattle on a thousand hills. I'm just a mom-and-pop businessman trying to get on my feet and make an honest living. And the Lord needs my mule. How many mules are there within a few furlongs of here and He picks me! Oh, who am I to question!"

He turned to the man, "Take it. You'd better go!"

"What can we pay you?"

"You must pay nothing. If I take your gold, I would only have to claim it and report the sale. If Herod is coming, he will certainly stop here and ask questions. If you ever return, you can make it right. Now go. Leave quickly. It will be trouble enough for me if they find you here. I would rather lose a good mule than lose my livelihood . . . or worse. My first day! Go!"

Sol helped them change mounts and gave them some pomegranates for their journey. As they turned to go, the young man handed him the vial of myrrh.

"Keep this until we return, and may God be with you."

"And with you," Sol said as he took the vial. He watched them disappear into the night, then he kicked the dirt and threw the tent flap down in disgust. "This is no way to start a business. Donkey King! Huh! More like mule-faced fool!" He knew he would never see them again. And he doubted even more that he would ever make sense of the conversation he just had. "Some young kid and his girl just sweet-talked me out of a good profit!"

He closed up the tent, watered the animals, and headed slowly home. Sneaking in to bed so as to not wake his wife (and not have to explain), he slept better than he had in years.

And the years went by. Sol's business actually grew. He eventually sold the lot outside of Bethlehem and bought some property in a choice location to the north of Jerusalem. Traffic was heavier there.

His wife bore him four sons. They grew up, married, gave him four beautiful daughters-in-law and grand-children. Everything was going well. Everyone in the region knew him as the Donkey King. His sons had learned the trade and were taking on more responsibility. Sol was looking forward to retirement. And then trouble came.

Small business owners had always been taxed unfairly, but now Sol had been falsely accused of failing to accurately report inventory over the previous six years. The audit itself took the better part of a year. In the meantime, his assets were frozen and he lost everything. He lost his animals, his property, and all his savings. He had nothing. Retirement was out of the question. His sons had to move west to the coast to find work.

Determined to rebuild, and despite his age, Sol hired himself out as a brick maker and a wheat thresher. His wife took in laundry and wove baskets. In a year's time, they saved enough to buy a sturdy donkey, a female - a breeder. What is more, just three weeks after he bought her he found out she was carrying a foal.

"Praise be to God!" he shouted. The Lord had

provided. The Donkey King would come back stronger than ever!

The animal gave birth to a healthy female, and Sol kept working. Within a year, he figured he could re-open for business.

It was the week before Passover, and Sol's wife was getting the house ready for out-of-town guests, relatives coming down from Tyre.

Sol and his wife lived on the main road at the north edge of Bethphage. Traffic was getting heavy as the holiday approached. Sol normally kept his two animals in the back. To be safe, however, he decided to keep them tied up by the front door where he could keep an eye on them. He kept his dog there to warn him of any thieves.

Passover week arrived. Crowds that had settled in on the Sabbath were starting to move again. Most didn't travel on the Sabbath. They didn't clean up after themselves either. The road was a mess. Makeshift campsites were all along the thoroughfare. Sol and his wife were just sitting down to breakfast, when they heard the dog barking out by the front door. Sol jumped up from the table, grabbed a stick he kept by the door and ran outside to see what it was. He was surprised to find two young men untying the knots on the ropes to his donkey and foal.

"What do you think you're doing? Take your hands off my animals!" he shouted, coming after them with the stick raised above his head.

The two men backed off, raised their hands, looked at each other with surprise and said, "Whoa! Hold on sir! We were not intending to steal them. We were told to come get them. We're sorry. We should have asked first."

"Who told you to take them?" He kept his stick raised. "Are you with the temple guard?" They didn't look like police. They looked foreign and they weren't armed.

"Oh no!" they smiled nervously. "We are only here for the Passover. We're from Galilee."

"Then what business do you have with my donkeys?"

The men looked at each other, then looked at Sol, just as surprised as he was. "It is the Lord. He has need of them."

"What! The Lord has need of them?" Sol raised his stick, then felt the blood drain from his arms. "The Lord has need of them?" The words pierced through his defenses.

"The Lord has need of them? But they are all I have." Sol was feeling queasy, suddenly not so steady on his feet.

His legs went wobbly. "The Lord asks for my life."

The men looked at each other, then broke out in laughter, not in ridicule, but as if they understood completely.

"What are you laughing at?" Sol asked. He was not feeling well at all. "There are other animals in town. Why does he want mine?"

The men shrugged, and with a bit of empathy said, "We are doing only as he told us."

Sol, still catching his breath, rubbed the neck of the donkey and shook his head. "You old soft-hearted fool," he whispered.

"I suppose you don't know when you'll be back?"

The men slowly shook their heads. "All we were told to tell you is, 'The Lord has need of them.'"

Sol looked up at the sky, squinted, and shook his head. "The Lord has need of them." Where had he heard that before? He closed his eyes and dropped the stick. He felt as if he had lived this moment before, perhaps in another life, like he was in a play and was acting out a role that had been written for him. He had an uneasy sense of what his lines were supposed to be.

While the men held the rope, Sol rubbed the muzzle of the donkey, stroked the young colt, paused, and then something came out of his mouth that had to have come from somewhere else.

"Take them. Take good care of them. They're all I have."

The men thanked him graciously, untied the donkeys and walked back up the hill against the traffic. Sol slowly entered the house. His wife was standing at the door, staring at him in disbelief, but he just walked by her, waving her off. "Don't even ask," he said. He didn't feel like eating and he went back to bed.

As the sun grew hot, the crowds picked up. The road was jammed with people, animals for travel, animals for food, and animals for sacrifice. Children were running everywhere. Then beyond the normal commotion, their rose a tremendous shout just beyond the hill to the north. Sol and his wife ran out the door to see what it was. The noise was deafening. It was the sound of singing and shouting. In the middle of the throng was a man on a donkey with a foal tied behind. Sol recognized them as his animals.

The people were celebrating and singing praises. The songs were about the long-awaited Messiah. "Could it be?"

Sol wondered. "Any man on a donkey didn't look much like a king." Not only that, but this man looked distracted, even sad. As he got closer, Sol could tell he had been weeping. What an odd sight, and yet there was something unusual about the man. There was a quiet authority about him.

Then Sol thought of the oddest thing. The thought grew to a firm resolve. He dashed into the house. "It must still be here. I know I just saw it a few days ago." He ran to the back room, uncovered an old trunk, under some blankets and some old parchments. There it was! He grabbed the vial and ran out the door, just as the crowd pressed by. He couldn't get close to the man on the donkey, but he caught his eye. The man smiled. Sol ran ahead and gave the vial of myrrh to some women who were with his entourage. Then for whatever reason – what had come over him? - Sol took off his cloak and threw it on the ground, just in time for his own donkey to trample all over it. "I've completely lost it," he thought. He caught himself weeping and laughing as he said it.

Opportunities to obey come often on any given day. The call to a profound obedience, however, may come only once in a lifetime. And when it comes, it is a wise and discerning person who recognizes it for what it is, and acts accordingly.

It does little good to question. If obedience were merely a private matter, affecting only what is ours, we could hope to explore and evaluate every angle of the thing. But when our obedience plays into a larger story, we can only know in part. So we are called to obey, even when to do so goes against the current of good reason and common sense.

And so it was with the Donkey King, who watched the unlikely King on his donkey until he disappeared inside the city gate. Sol turned around, ignored the trash in his yard, went inside and washed. He grabbed a pomegranate, then went back outside to sit in front of his house, watch the crowds, and think.

That night, he retired early and tossed and turned in his bed, thinking about the man on the donkey. Who was he? What was it about him that seemed so familiar? Tomorrow he would have to go and find out for himself. Yes, that is what he would do.

He lay awake for the longest time, thinking about everything and then thinking about nothing in particular.

And when sleep finally came, Sol rested better than he had in years.

Stupid Gift
Christmas Eve, 2006

When I was a kid, growing up in Dearborn, MI, our family opened presents on Christmas Eve. I don't know why we did it that way, but I never complained. We had to wait until after the Christmas Eve service at our Free Methodist Church. We wanted to go, but even if we didn't want to, we would have had to go because my dad was the pastor.

The parsonage was next door to the church, only a few feet from the side door. We'd rush home, beside ourselves with excitement. The doorbell would ring constantly as church members dropped by one more small gift, a candle, plate of cookies, or another fruit cake. We were rich, and all the world was right on this night.

Most of the presents had incubated under the tree for a while. Two weeks earlier, my dad had loaded everyone into the station wagon and we all went to the K-Mart over on Van Born. It was a family ritual. My older brother Paul, who was ten, and I were each allotted five dollars to spend. I was eight years old. My sister, Carol, was five. She tagged along with my mother. My youngest brother, Steve, was three. He just rode in my Dad's cart and pulled stuff off the shelves.

Paul and I each secured our own shopping carts, then we took off through the store, sneaking down this aisle and that, keeping ourselves aware of where the other was. The game was that you had to make your way around the store and through the checkout line without being seen until everything was paid for and safely bagged up. More often than not, it didn't work. I'd turn a corner and run right into my brother's cart. We'd accuse each other of spying, then speed off in opposite directions.

It was odd how often we ended up getting each other the same thing, or variations of the same thing. I don't know if it was that we were brothers, or if I was just not so original. The previous year, I bought Paul a *Bat Masterson* 45 rpm record. It cost forty-nine cents. Bat Masterson was a TV western hero who carried a cane, wore a vested suit, and derby hat. He beat up bad guys with his cane without getting his suit dirty and shot guns out of their hands with a tiny derringer pistol he kept in his vest pocket. *"His name was Bat, Bat Masterson."*

Paul bought me a 45 rpm record as well. It was *Babes in Toyland.* Not quite the same. For several weeks after Christmas, I listened to the *Bat Masterson* record quite a bit. I don't remember listening to the *Babes in Toyland* record. I thought it was my brother's plot to keep me a little kid for another year.

The previous spring, we both had discovered plastic model kits. I had built my first model car that I bought with birthday money. It was a model of the roadster that the TV Munsters drove. It ended up with airplane glue blotched all over it, but it was mine and I was proud of it. Paul had built a couple model cars too.

I headed over to the hobby section. They had model cars, planes, motorcycles, and boats. The boxes were stacked eight feet high. I couldn't spend much. I noticed a small model of a battleship for $1.49. That was perfect, so I bought it.

My Dad liked chocolate covered cherries. Those were easy.

Mom was a bit harder to buy for. I remembered something she said back on Thanksgiving. She announced to no one in particular that she needed a new can opener. I was in the kitchen when she said it. My dad was there too, and when we heard her say it, his eyes met mine and he kind of winked. That's what I would get for her, a new can opener.

I wheeled around to find the kitchen supply section, ran into my brother again, said a few choice words, then made my way to the can openers. They had a basket full of nice shiny ones, the kind where you clamped down on a can and then turn a little handle until the top came off. The handles had grips like pliers, so you could crack nuts with them. It looked like it worked real good, and it was only $1.19. She would love it.

For Carol, I found a little doll that had a hole in its mouth where you stuck a bottle of water and then it all came out the bottom. I thought she'd like that.

I bought Steve a toy car that if you rolled it backwards on the carpet about three feet real fast then let it go, it would go forward all by itself for about a foot. It was a bargain at .39 cents.

I was the first through the checkout, with my bag of gifts in hand, sitting by the front door. I was rather pleased with myself as I waited for my slow family.

We got home and went to separate rooms to wrap our bounty, then slid them under the tree. My wrapping technique required inordinate amounts of tape and paper, but I did it all by myself.

Christmas Eve couldn't come fast enough. The service

ended at 8:00. By 8:05 we were home, changed into our pajamas, and waiting for my dad. He had taken his time greeting the last of the folks at church. He had to turn out the lights, stop by his office, and lock up. Pastors were like sea captains – the last one off the ship. Finally, we heard him coming through the back door. He ran in and got a fire started, then had to hurry back to the church office for something, then the phone rang.

We were all still in our places around the living room when Dad finally returned and settled in. He got the Bible out and read the Christmas story to us, then the book of Isaiah, then we had to have prayer. I didn't mind, really. Our family always prayed before something important, and I couldn't think of anything more important than opening Christmas presents.

Finally, we were ready for the main event. Mom laid out the ground rules. We'd have to take turns. My older brother got to be Santa Claus. He distributed the packages one at a time, youngest to the oldest, while my mother wrote down who got what and from whom on a little spiral notebook. That was for thank-you notes later on.

I had studied every present under the tree for days. I lifted them, shook them, smelled them, and pressed down on the wrapping to see if I could see any letters or pictures through the paper. I never succeeded, but that didn't stop me from trying.

We always started with the lame stuff – pajamas, slippers, Vitalis hair tonic, soap on a rope - stuff that I could do without. They were things that, say, if you were to be dropped off on a deserted island, and you could only take a few items with you, they would not be at the top of your list.

Eventually, we got to the better stuff, the presents we siblings got each other. I opened my present from my brother. It was a small model kit of a navy submarine. Pretty cool.

I reached under the tree to get the present I bought for him. It felt kind of warm. Paul began opening it. I couldn't wait to see the look of surprise on his face. He tore off the paper, looked at the picture on the front, then opened the box, then he looked back at the picture. His face scrunched up and he gave me a funny look. He reached in the box and pulled out the hull of the model boat. It was warped and bent out of shape.

It didn't take me long to figure it out. After I had wrapped his present, I had placed it under the tree, but right over the heat register. There it sat for two weeks.

Paul stuffed the melted pieces back in the box and I heard him whisper under his breath, "Stupid present!" I don't know if I heard him say it, or if the words originated in my head. Either way, it was true. It was stupid. I felt bad. I was stupid. What was I thinking? All that money gone to waste, and K-Mart would never take it back. I'd try to make it up to him next year.

It was my mom's turn next. She had gotten a candy dish from somebody, a new set of dishcloths, and now my brother pulled out a bigger box and laid it in her lap. It was from my dad. She opened it with the same line she'd always say, "Well, what could this be? I hope you didn't spend too much Frank!" It was a white box with a picture and some printing on it.

As she was unwrapping the paper, I could pick out the block red letters on the box. They read, "E-L-E-C-T-R-I-C C-A-N O-P-E-N-E-R." It was a fancy one, the kind that you mount under the wall cabinet. You plug it in and just slip the can in under the handle and press down and it turns all on its own like magic and the lid comes off clean. There was even a little slot with a sharp blade in it to open bags of chips and stuff.

It was magnificent.

She let out a sigh and a big thank you to my dad. "Oh Frank, you shouldn't have!" He was obviously pleased with himself. I wanted to crawl under the couch.

I looked to see where my can opener was. It was still under the tree. I recognized it by the wrapping – red and green wrinkled paper with Christmas trees all over it. My can opener didn't come in a box. It was an odd shaped thing that was hard to wrap, so I used a lot of paper and loads of tape.

After we went around again, it was my mom's turn. My brother reached way back under the tree and retrieved my present for her. She held it and looked it over. "Well, what could this be? I hope you didn't spend a lot of money!" "No problem there," I thought to myself. All of a sudden, I wasn't so excited about Christmas.

Mom carefully unwrapped the rolls of paper and tape. It took her awhile. When she finally laid eyes on it, she opened her mouth wide in feigned surprise. The room was quiet, until my brother reared back, kicked his legs in the air, and let out a whoop. "It's another can opener!"

He didn't have to say any more. In fact, I don't think he said anything more, but I heard it. I heard it in my head - that same voice. Was it my brother's voice? Or my voice? Or from somewhere else? Either way, the words burned deep, "Stupid present."

My mom looked at me tenderly. She was good at that. She said, "Oh thank you, Mark!" And I knew that she knew what I was thinking as I mustered a sheepish half smile. "I think this will be perfect to take to the cottage, then we'll have one up there too!" She was good at that too – making a bad situation seem not so bad, but I knew the truth. It was a stupid gift. I was outmaneuvered by my own dad. He had more money than me. I was terrible at Christmas.

Well, before you, the reader, grow too concerned about my fragile psyche, it's important for me to tell you that I eventually got over it. Life went on.

Over the years, however, there were other things, other times when I heard that same voice, the voice that we all hear from time to time.

None of us are really sure of ourselves. We've blown it lots of times, said or done a stupid thing, or worse. And we have all said or done something that hurt someone. The guilt comes easily and it carries us away in waves.

"Stupid gift!" "Nice try!" "Loser!" The voices are constant. And there are times we deserve it, I suppose.

Our hearts are stained with the sludge of sin, cowardice, pride, lust, deception, and shame. We then cover them over with layers of shiny wrapping, held together with lots of tape. Still our heavenly Father desires us. We are of no use to Him, yet he wants us for himself.

He wants to adopt us into His family, to make us His very own precious possession.

Being God, he could make us come to him. He could force us to obey Him, but then that wouldn't be love. He desires children, not slaves or robots. He desires our hearts, but only as a freely offered gift.

The very moment, however, when we think of giving ourselves to him, a voice hisses in our head, "Stupid present!" But the Lord looks at the soiled, shriveled, warped, and broken offering of our lives, and he says lovingly, "I'll take it." And he cherishes it most of all.

So, what do you give a big God who has everything?

What can I give Him, poor as I am?
If I were a shepherd, I would give a lamb
If I were a wiseman, I would do my part
What I can I give him, give him my heart.

Virtual Reality
Christmas Eve, 2007

Jeff Strobel made his first of several million by the age
of twenty-seven. He was now an investment advisor for the
pension boards of several for-profit and non-profit
organizations. He also managed the portfolios of several
wealthy clients. He was nearing thirty-five. He and his wife,
Meg, lived in an upscale community north of Chicago.
They had one daughter, five-year-old Marnie.

Meg had wanted more kids, but Jeff insisted that one
was enough. He hardly had enough time for a family of
three. He had worked hard to build up an elite clientele.
His job used to take him out of town often, but now,
except for three or four trips a year, he worked mostly out
of his office. It was a suite he had built over their four-bay
garage. He spent most of his time out there, trading by
day, contacting clients, and doing research late into the
night. He didn't have many friends and didn't get out
much. He lived in front of his computer screen.

He and Meg had been married nine years. It's not that
their relationship was bad or anything. He did love her
and he was faithful to her. It's just that she had her life and

he had his. As too often happens to married people, they had slowly drifted apart. Most of Meg's time was taken up with Marnie's private pre-K academy, dance lessons, multi-sensory art classes, soccer practice, and play dates.

Sometime in October, after soccer season, Meg started saying something about the need to balance their lives with some kind of spirituality, so she enrolled herself and Marnie in a yoga class and then, of all things, started taking her to a kids' program at a church near the mall.

She asked Jeff if he wanted to come to church with them, but he flatly said "No." He told her that most churches were full of naïve people who couldn't think for themselves, so they fell for make-believe religion. "It's all fake," he would say. Besides, Sunday was the only day he could sleep in and have a day just for himself. Meg told him that she thought that was funny because it seemed that he lived every day for himself and that maybe Sunday should be a day for somebody else, like his wife and daughter for example, or maybe God.

He told her to give him a break and who else was going to work to make the income that they needed to live like they did. She just rolled her eyes, walked away and never brought it up again, which he had gotten used to, and then he didn't think about it much either.

As autumn gave way to colder weather, Jeff was feeling old and puffy. The weight came on gradually. He had tried exercise, at least for a while. In a spare room next to his office suite he had a full universal gym installed plus a step machine, a stationary bike, a treadmill and an elliptical, but he had a hard time staying with it. It was all rather boring.

Then, back in November, at a trade show in Las Vegas, he saw a demonstration of a Virtual Game Explorer VRX III. It was a virtual reality entertainment system. It was a full-body sensory thing that cost as much as his parents paid for their first house. Being the early adapter that he was, he bought one. He didn't have space in his office suite, so he had to have it delivered and set up temporarily in the family room at the house. He told Meg that he would figure out a place for it later.

It came with a black body suit covered with dozens of strategically placed sensors and panels. They included temperature controllers and tiny air-driven impact pistons that could re-create contact, or even collision anywhere in the body. In a boxing game, if you were hit in the stomach, you'd really feel it. It had an 8x8' platform and also a suspended harness for flying or swimming. The gloves and shoes were fitted with numerous sensors as well. The system came with a wand that could serve as any number of implements – a golf club, baseball bat, hockey stick, harpoon, hunting rifle, etc.

The key feature was the visor and helmet which completely encompassed the head except for the nose and mouth. It featured surround-sound digital audio and the latest rendering of HD display with a 360-degree visual field that at any position offered 200 degrees periphery and 100 degrees vertical, equal to the human eye. It had a small microphone for interactive voice commands. The helmet was fitted with hundreds of sensory electrodes that actually read increases in skin temperature and pulse. The system specs even claimed it could pick up certain brain waves.

In time, the computer could learn to anticipate responses. It came with a warning in fine print in the instructions that said that, though no incidents had as yet been recorded, their remained a conceptual possibility that the system could result in a temporary separation of the subject's brain from their body. "Oh great!" said Meg when he told her. "You don't need a machine to help you do that!"

The system's sensory potential stimulated sight, sound, temperature, and impact. The more expensive upgrades included smell, but that's where Meg drew the line.

It took Jeff some time to get the hang of it. It was like learning to walk again. It actually involved exercise. At least that's how Jeff rationalized it to Meg.

It didn't feature "games," but rather what the system called "experiences." It came bundled with a few samples. Some of them were pretty interesting. One was called "Virtual Applause." It was just a short thing where you walked out onto a spot lit stage in a large arena filled with 80,000 people who stood and clapped and screamed your name for as long as you wanted.

Another one was "Traffic Jam." You pick one of 10 major metropolitan areas in the world. You start out in bumper to bumper traffic, but you could slam into cars, cut people off, and make meaningful gestures to other drivers as you fought your way out. He found it to be pretty therapeutic after a long day of work.

One was called "Virtual Family Meal." You sat at a virtual dinner table with a virtual wife and two virtual kids. Your wife would smile at you and tell you how wonderful you were and ask you only interesting questions about your work, your plans, and your dreams. Your two virtual children would dress nice and practice good manners and ask you questions about history, geography and etiquette.

Jeff was spending more and more time on the VRXIII.

It was Christmas Eve. The church by the Mall was having their children's program. Marnie was invited to sing in the kids' choir and she wanted to go. The previous Saturday, Meg had asked Jeff if he would go to the church with them. He was noncommittal. She asked him again that evening as she was helping Marnie get dressed. It was already 6:00 and the program started at 7:00. He was strapped into his VRXIII, sitting in on a jazz combo, when Meg came into the room and tapped on his helmet. He slipped it off to hear her in mid-sentence ask him if he was going. "Going where?" he asked.

"To the church program!"

He told her he had worked all day and was tired. "You go ahead. I think I'll sit this one out. Maybe I'll wrap a few more presents and bake some brownies before you get back."

Meg was about to say something, then decided it wasn't worth it. She just looked at him, clamped her lips shut, then turned away and ushered Marnie out the door.

Jeff put his helmet on and went back to the jazz combo. Then he thought he'd hunt buffalo in the old west for a while, then off to a boxing match in Manilla, then snowboarding in the Alps.

He was snorkeling in the Bahamas when everything suddenly went black.

Jeff slowly raised his visor. The whole house was dark. There wasn't any light coming from the street lamps outside either. Suddenly, a small, alien-looking being appeared in the room. The creature was illuminated by an eerie light emanating upwards, revealing a frightening countenance with dark shadows that outlined a ghastly face. The light then turned towards Jeff, blinding him. He squinted, shielded his eyes, and cautiously asked, "Who are you?"

"I'm Marnie, your daughter." She pulled the flashlight back to her face.

"Did you unplug me?"

"Mommy said there's been a storm."

Jeff could hear the wind and sleet hitting the window.

He pulled off his helmet, slipped out of the harness, and undid his body suit. "Get out of Daddy's way Pumpkin while I go out and get the generator going."

Marnie didn't move. She flashed the light back into his eyes and said, "Read me a story."

He gently turned the light back into Marnie's face and looked down at his persistent five-year-old. She wasn't going to move. He could tell this was serious. She looked more like her mother every day.

"O.K." he sighed. "I suppose for a minute. What d'ya got?"

She held out a book. It was an old hard-bound volume. The red cover was worn and some of the pages were taped together. "Alright," he said. "For just a minute or two." He stretched and let out a yawn. Marnie stretched and yawned too, then grabbed his hand and pulled him over to the couch, turned, and pushed him down into the seat cushion. She bounded up next to him, jumped into his lap, and presented the book. "You read and I'll turn the pages," she demanded.

"Sounds like a plan," he said.

The cover had a rather droll title, "Bible Story Book". Marnie opened to a bookmark somewhere in the middle, then rubbed her palm along the crease. It wasn't necessary. The book was worn and looked like it had been opened to that page many times before. Jeff cleared his throat. Marnie cleared her throat. Then he began:

*"And it came to pass in those days, that there went out
a decree from Caesar Augustus that all the world should
be taxed."*

The pages were soft and had yellowed slightly. Despite
its age, Jeff was struck with the beauty of the pictures.
They were quality gloss prints of hand-painted illustrations
combined with classic works of art. He continued.

*"And all went to be taxed, every one into his own city.
And Joseph also went up from Galilee, out of the city of
Nazareth, into Judea, unto the city of David, which is
called Bethlehem; (because he was of the house and
lineage of David) to be taxed with Mary his espoused wife,
who was great with child. "*

"What's a lineage?" Marnie asked.

"I think it meant what family he belonged to. Like,
you are I are of the lineage of Strobel."

She looked up at him and giggled, then snuggled deep,
leaning her head back into his neck. She curled her tiny
hand around his thumb. She had just had a bath. Her
fingers were cool and pruney. Her soft hair brushed
against his cheek. It had the delicate scent of baby
shampoo.

Across the page was a picture of Joseph with Mary on

a donkey, weary travelers on a lonely road.

Marnie wasn't in a hurry. She looked at the picture for a long time, soaking in every detail before she turned the page.

"And so it was, that, while they were there, the days were accomplished that she should be delivered. And she brought forth her firstborn son, and wrapped him in swaddling clothes, and laid him in a manger; because there was no room for them in the inn."

The next picture showed Mary and Joseph sitting quietly in the warm light of a stable full of animals. In the center was the baby in the manger.

"Daddy, what's a manger?" Marnie asked as she rubbed the ridges on his thumbnail.

"Well, if I remember right, it's a box where the animals got their food."

Marnie looked at the picture and sat quietly. She was thinking. Jeff could sense the gears in her little brain turning. "Stop a second Daddy. Don't move. I'll be right back." Before he could ask her where she was going, she was off the couch and gone. He watched her little legs carry her full speed out of the room. She never just walked anywhere.

A minute later, she was back. She climbed back into his lap, grabbed the book, and opened to the same page. "Have to go to the bathroom?" He asked. "No," she said. She leaned back against his neck and grabbed his thumb again. "Read!" she demanded as she pressed her index finger to the page.

"And there were in the same country shepherds abiding in the field, keeping watch over their flock by night. And, lo, the angel of the Lord came upon them, and the glory of the Lord shone round about them: and they were sore afraid."

She gently traced the picture with her fingers. There were five shepherds kneeling with sheep all around and a deep blue night sky filled with stars. One lone bright light shone high in the heavens.

"And the angel said unto them, 'Fear not: for, behold, I bring you good tidings of great joy, which shall be to all people. For unto you is born this day in the city of David a Savior, which is Christ the Lord. And this shall be a sign unto you; Ye shall find the babe wrapped in swaddling clothes, lying in a manger.'"

He turned the page this time. The picture showed a magnificent angel, looking so lifelike and threatening, standing tall among the shepherds. The angel's arms were muscular and his hair was golden and his eyes were fierce. He wasn't anything like those chubby little ceramic angels that Meg had placed on the fireplace mantle, the ones she got at the New Age store.

Marnie was quiet for a moment, then without looking up, she asked, "Are angels real Daddy?" Jeff looked at her and wasn't sure what to say. "I don't know, sweetheart. I'd like to think that they are."

"They're real," she said emphatically, yawned, then turned the page.

"And suddenly there was with the angel a multitude of the heavenly host praising God, and saying, 'Glory to God in the highest, and on earth peace, good will toward men.'"

The picture showed the same night sky ablaze with angels. The shepherds were on their faces, pounding the earth with joy. Or were they clutching the ground in fear? Jeff couldn't tell. He wondered how he would respond if he were there. Would he welcome the angel's message or would he be overcome with terror?

He noticed Marnie was quiet. He could feel her body rise and fall ever so slightly in cadence with her shallow breathing. She was so still, fully relaxed in his arms. He felt her heartbeat against his chest. She had fallen asleep.

He thought he would close the book, maybe get up, get the generator going. He couldn't go back to snorkeling.

The generator wasn't powerful enough to run the VRXIII.

Meg had gone around and lit an old kerosene lamp and some candles. Jeff thought he'd get up, but he didn't. Maybe in a minute. He realized he didn't want to lose this moment.

He looked again at the front and then the back of the book, when it dawned on him where he had seen it before. It was his book. It was one he had as a little boy. It was the one that his mother had read to him on many nights before she tucked him into bed, until his daddy left and the divorce happened. It was the book that his mother had told him that her own father had read to her.

It all came back to him - the words, the pictures – the memories of his mother and bedtimes and Christmases past.

He knew this story. He flipped back to the beginning and traced the pictures. He remembered. He came back to where he left off and turned the page.

"And it came to pass, as the angels were gone away from them into heaven, the shepherds said one to another, 'Let us now go even unto Bethlehem, and see this thing which is come to pass, which the Lord hath made known unto us.' And they came with haste, and found Mary, and Joseph, and the babe lying in a manger."

The picture showed the stable with the shepherds bowing low before the manger. Mary and Joseph were very still. A light shown around the baby, wrapped in cloth, and lying in the manger.

"And when they had seen it, they made known everywhere the saying which was told them concerning this child. And all they that heard it wondered at those things which were told them by the shepherds."

The picture showed the shepherds running through the town, with some sheep following them. They were pointing back in the direction of the stable, tears streaming down their faces. There were people in the street. Jeff noticed that some in the picture were listening. Others seemed to be mocking. A little child in a doorway hung on every word, while a shopkeeper standing nearby paid no attention as he swept the floor.

Jeff brushed back Marnie's hair from his face and studied the picture. He remembered it, but still it all seemed so new to him.

"But Mary kept all these things, and pondered them in her heart. And the shepherds returned, glorifying and praising God for all the things that they had heard and seen, as it was told unto them."

Jeff turned to the back pages of the book to find a picture of Jesus stretched out on a cross. There was blood streaming down his thorn-gashed head and blood oozing from the nail holes in his hands and feet. The pictures were graphic. They struck him with such force, even angered him. "Why would anyone put this in a children's book? It's far too real." he thought. "They would never do this today."

And then, across the last page, on the inside back cover, was a final picture of Jesus, alive, strong, muscular, with his wild hair blowing in the wind and standing on the clouds with his hands extended. In each outstretched hand were the nail wounds.

Jeff closed the book, and studied the front cover again. It smelled musty. The binding looked as if it would fall apart if it were opened many more times. "Where did Marnie find this?" He hugged her tight and pressed his cheek against hers. The flashlight was going out.

Jeff sat quiet on the couch in the dark. He was far away, and yet struck suddenly by a sobering awareness that life here and now was flying by pretty fast, and he was in danger of missing it. In his own house, Jeff was lost in his thoughts, or was it that maybe his thoughts were finding him?

"Are angels real?" he wondered. "Are you real?" he half prayed, not expecting anyone to answer. And yet the question haunted him, awakening his senses and stirring some deep part of him that had long gone unopened and nearly forgotten, like this musty old picture book.

Then from the kitchen came Meg's voice. She burst into the family room with a candle in hand, laughing. "Who wrapped a baby doll in my good hand towel and put it in the cat dish?"

Rich People
Christmas Eve, 2009

Liza Harden went downstairs to check the mail. She was hoping it had come early. December had arrived too quickly for her. Her four oldest were back in school after Thanksgiving break. There was fourteen-year-old Maggie, twelve-year-old Molly, nine-year-old Mindy, and six-year-old Amanda. And then there was Orton, her only boy, who was three. He was named after his grandfather.

Liza's husband Ed had died shortly after Orton was born. It happened this time of year, with the first winter storm. It was an accident. Ed worked for a garage and towing company and was working all night pulling people out of snowbanks. On the way home just before dawn, he hit some black ice, went off the road, hit a guard rail, flipped the car into a bridge abutment, and then he was gone.

Ed had only enough life insurance to pay for a modest funeral. He left Liza with $1,800 in savings, a baby and four girls to raise. She had to give up the house they had been renting and move with the kids into a smaller apartment above the laundromat on 2nd street. She talked the rent down with the owner by agreeing to tidy up the place every evening and do a deep cleaning once a week.

She also convinced him to let her use the laundry for free and also if he would leave the heat ducts open underneath her apartment to allow heat from the laundromat to circulate upstairs. She unscrewed the floor vent covers so the warm air would come up to where they lived. The machines down below were noisy, and it was still cold, but it was bearable.

Liza worked as many jobs as she could. In addition to cleaning the laundromat, she ran the cash register at the Piggly Wiggly grocery store two blocks away. She took in laundry for people and on Fridays, watched three other babies besides her own. She kept a clean house and she fretted over her children. She helped them with their homework, taught them their manners, and took them to church every Sunday.

The little Baptist church was two blocks away. The older ones helped the younger ones get ready. They all were proud of their Sunday dresses. They felt like princesses as they walked to Sunday School. They didn't notice some of the other children whispering about them, about how they always wore the same thing every week.

The girls loved church, and they came home particularly excited the Sunday before Advent when Pastor Moore announced that the entire church was going to work together to take a special offering for a poor family that Christmas. He described the family as having gone through some rough times, and deserving of help, and that this was the season for giving, and could everyone go home and save some extra money to bring with them in three weeks, the third Sunday of Advent. He didn't let on who the family might be.

The girls came home chattering like birds about what they were going to do to raise money for the poor family's Christmas. Maggie got some babysitting jobs. She sold an old Barbie and Ken doll to a friend at school for five dollars. When it snowed Friday night, Molly and Mindy went out the next morning, knocking on doors of houses and shops to shovel what seemed like miles of sidewalks. Their rate was fifty cents per section of walk. Maggie took them all out every evening before dinner to go scrounging for pop cans.

Amanda and Orton went downstairs in the mornings before school to check under chairs, around the washers and dryers, and even the popcorn machine, looking for loose change. Orton's hands were small enough where he could wiggle a finger under the machines.

It wasn't unusual for him to flush out a nickel or a dime or a quarter. One time Amanda found a whole dollar bill. Another time Orton found a stick of gum under a dryer. It was still in the wrapper, but his mother made them throw it away.

Every night the girls were thrilled to put the change and dollar bills that they had gathered in a big jar. Liza agreed to throw in an extra two percent of her laundry work. This was on top of her regular tithe. Every night the jar got heavier as it filled with crumpled bills and sticky pennies, nickels, dimes, and quarters.

As they admired their growing treasure, Mindy wondered aloud if perhaps they might have the biggest offering of anyone at their little church. Amanda blurted out confidently, "You got that right, Bub!"

It was a line she had picked up on the playground at school. She was wearing it out, as far as her mother was concerned. Liza calmly reminded Amanda that she should address people by their real name.

Before bed every night, they all prayed for the poor family who was going to have the best Christmas ever.

The three weeks sped by. The Friday evening before the special Sunday offering, they dumped the change and bills on the kitchen table to count it. It came to $87.48. They still had some work to do the next day. Molly had to feed Mr. Sheets', their neighbor's, cat while he was away overnight. Liza had gotten some extra Christmas tips at the grocery store. The others went downstairs to check the laundromat for loose change one more time. Before noon on Saturday, they rounded what they had to $100 and took the money to the bank. They asked for crisp new bills – four brand-new twenty-dollar bills and two tens. They put it all in an envelope and placed it in Liza's purse to be ready for the next day's offering.

The next morning was the third Sunday of Advent, a week and a half before Christmas. As always, they walked to church. It was cold, but they dressed warm and could think of nothing else but the offering that day. When the blessed moment arrived, Liza took out the envelope and gave each child a crisp new bill to put in the offering plate. A whole hundred dollars! They felt rich. What a Christmas this would be for a special family. After the offering the pastor thanked the people for their generosity and announced that they would be taking the Christmas gift to this needy family that very afternoon.

They walked home after church, ate their dinner and had all the dishes nearly put away when they heard a knock at the door downstairs. Maggie looked out the front window and saw a brown car that looked like Pastor Moore's Buick. Liza went down to answer it. The girls heard the door open, then some talking. It was a man's voice. It sounded like Pastor Moore. They heard their mother say "thank-you," then the door gently shut.

Liza come back up the stairs. She was walking very slowly, taking each step one at a time, not bounding up every other one like she sometimes did. She closed the door behind her and came into the kitchen. She had a smile on her face, but it looked like the kind of smile that was working to hide a very different feeling on the inside. The girls were full of questions. "What is it Momma?" "Was that Pastor Moore?" "What did he want?"

Liza sat down at the kitchen table and pulled out an envelope. "What is it?" the girls asked as they leaned in around her. Their mother laid the envelope on the table, took a breath, then slowly opened it. It was full of money. The girls bent closer and stared at it. Liza carefully spread it out. Maggie counted it. There were five $20 bills, eight $10 bills, seven $5's, twenty-one ones, twenty-six quarters, and some dimes, nickels, and pennies – $244.73.

Everyone looked at the pile of cash as if they weren't sure what it was. Not a word was spoken, but the truth slowly descended on each of them like a fog. So, they were the poor family that Pastor Moore was talking about this whole month in church. They all slumped back in their chairs and sat quietly. The children looked at their mother as they always did when needing guidance as to know what to think, and in times like this, what to feel.

Liza looked around at them, smiled sweetly and scanned the faces of each of her dear children. She drew a deep breath and said in a manufactured cheery voice, "Well, wasn't that nice of Pastor Moore and the church to give us this gift!"

Maggie, the oldest, had seen her mother like this before. Liza was good at putting a positive spin on most any situation. She had handled disappointment many times, and her words were her feeble but earnest attempt to comfort her children. At times she felt so inadequate as a mother, so helpless in her ability to redirect the pain and the confusion that so often threatened to erode the confidence and joy in her children's hearts.

So, they were poor after all. Maggie felt the blood drain from her chest. She still had her Sunday dress on. She dropped her chin, looked down and pulled at the hem. The dress was a deep royal blue print dress adorned with small golden flowers. She used to love that dress. Now it just looked old.

Liza straightened up in her chair, gathered up the money and put it all back in the envelope. "Well, that's just fine," she said with a smile. "We will figure out what to do with it tomorrow."

The rest of the day went rather quietly. The girls all stayed close to the apartment. The older ones didn't feel like doing much and the younger ones didn't want to play in the snow. The next day, they balked at going to school. One of them might have gotten away with it, but when all of them complained of having a belly ache, Liza got wise to them and got them moving, dressed, with books and lunches in their hands and out the door.

The days were different now. There was no going downstairs to the laundry to look for lost change, no babysitting, no interest in going out to shovel snow or look for pop cans. The girls quietly did their homework and didn't talk much, even at the dinner table. All that week, no one mentioned the envelope with the money in it.

Sunday came around. The girls didn't want to go to church. Maggie pleaded with her mother, protesting that she didn't have anything to wear. The others dragged their feet, but Mary made them all go.

They walked to church as they always did. After Sunday School, they joined their mother in the same row where they normally sat. There was a guest missionary speaker that morning. He was from a hard-to-pronounce faraway place called Myanmar. He showed pictures of a devastating typhoon that hit the country and told how many people had died. Those who survived didn't have enough food. What stores of rice they had were being eaten by hordes of rats that had been flushed out by the flooding. It sounded like a horror movie. The girls leaned forward, hanging on every word.

The missionary said that most of the people in Myanmar had never seen a Bible. They had never heard of Christmas. They did not know the story of Jesus in the manger. They had never heard of Bethlehem, or Mary and Joseph, or the shepherds and the wise men.

He reminded the little congregation of a verse that everyone at the little Baptist church knew by heart - John 3:16. Most of the people in this particular region of Myanmar did not know that "God so loved the world that he gave his only Son, that whoever believes in him will not perish but have everlasting life." He said that Myanmar was an important part of the world that God loved so much. The missionary talked about how Jesus purposely made himself poor so he could reach everyone with the good news that he was the Son of God.

He preached and then he prayed and sat down. The room was quiet. Then Pastor Moore came to the pulpit and said that they all had so much to be thankful for and that he felt the Lord was telling him to take a special offering for the missionary and for the people in Myanmar. It would help the churches there to buy rice and Bibles to take to the people who were suffering so much. "Could we all be generous this Christmas?" Pastor Moore asked wistfully. "Can we be as generous with our brothers and sisters in Myanmar as Christ has been generous with us?"

The kids' eyes opened wide and their mouths dropped open. They all turned at the same time and looked to their mother. She looked back at them and smiled. They were all thinking the same thing. She reached into her purse, took out the yellow envelope, and opened it. She gave each of the children a fistful of cash and coins to put in the offering as it went by - all $244.73 of it.

The plate made its way down the row. The kids were giddy as they put their offering in. They tried their best to hide it in their little hands so no one could see. Their pew was shaking with their excitement.

After the offering, the ushers took the plates away to

count it. The little congregation stood to sing the Doxology and then there were some announcements. Finally, an usher came forward and gave an envelope to the pastor. He looked at it briefly, chuckled, and then presented it to the missionary. "Go ahead, open it," Pastor Moore said.

The Missionary peeked at the contents in the envelope, pulled out the slip of white paper that was tucked inside and read it. His face broke into a look of utter surprise and then a wide smile. He held up a check and showed the congregation. "Four hundred and seventy-two dollars!" cried the Missionary. "This will help feed hundreds of children, help save their lives. It will also allow us to go into places where we've never been allowed before – to share with these dear people the good news of Jesus. Four hundred and seventy-two dollars! Just think of it! Thank you so much for your generosity!"

The Pastor closed the service with a prayer of thanksgiving. The organ launched into a rousing postlude of "Joy to the World." As people were filing out of their seats, Amanda made her way to the front to get a closer look at the missionary. As she approached, the guest speaker turned to Pastor Moore, shook his hand, and gushed, "What a remarkable offering for such a small congregation! Totally unannounced! What a blessing this is! You must have some wealthy folks around here!"

Amanda stepped between the two men, looked up, put her hands on her hips and bellowed, "You got that right, Bub!"

Mother Mary
Christmas Eve, 2011

Mary dropped six-year-old Zoe off at the back door of the First Methodist Church. It was an old white frame building on the corner of Second and Oak Street just a block off the town square. It was Saturday morning, the final rehearsal for the children's Christmas pageant to be performed the following Sunday evening at 6 p.m.

Mary was content not to go inside. She would wait for Zoe in the car. It had been twenty years since she had been to church, and it was this very church. She attended Sunday School there as a little girl. Her own family weren't much for religion. Her dad drank heavily and was in and out of the house. Her mother wasn't involved much in her life. Their neighbor, a kind lady named Mrs. Faust came over one day and asked her mother if it would be alright for Mary come to Sunday School with her. Nobody seemed to mind. Her parents would be asleep or hungover on most Sundays, so she went.

This went on for a year or so, and then Mary just stopped going. She couldn't remember why. Life just happened, and it happened for her pretty fast. She dropped out of school at sixteen, then within a month found out she was going to have a baby. It was a boy. She named him Devon. He would be fourteen now.

His father disappeared as soon as he found out Mary was expecting. Mary's mom told her not to bring a baby home, so the father's parents, who seemed like good people, took him in and pretty much raised him from the start. Mary gave up custody and signed adoption papers. The last she knew, they had moved somewhere out in Nevada about ten years ago. She's never heard from any of them again. She tried not to think about it too much, but she couldn't help wondering about him. Anyway, she was way too young at the time to worry about a baby. She didn't even have her driver's license.

Mary had been in several relationships after that - too many to count, but to no one really worth counting. She'd had two miscarriages, and then Zoe came along. Zoe's father promised to marry her, but life got a little too close for him and he joined the military, then got hired on with an oil pipeline crew up in Alaska. He'd send a little money once in a while, but that was about it. That left just the two of them. Zoe was six now. Where had the time gone?

Zoe was the light of Mary's life. She was growing up so fast. Mary also had to grow up in a hurry. She had to work three jobs - a part time job at Walmart, then a few hours a week as a waitress at the Three Chiefs Diner. She also cleaned houses on weekends when she could get them. On top of all this, she was working on her GED.

They got by, barely, but Mary wished she could do more for Zoe. Even though she'd pretty well messed up her own life, she was determined to do all she could to give Zoe what she never had – a loving mother who was around, decent clothes to wear, encouragement with her school-work, fix up a little bedroom she could call her own, and smother her with thousands of hugs and kisses.

The pageant practice was to last an hour and a half, so Mary decided to run to the store to buy some cards and run a few other errands. She got back to the church just in time for Zoe to come running out the side door. She was talking a mile a minute.

Zoe was a sweet girl, but Mary was hearing some things coming out of her mouth lately that scared her. A few months back she began thinking that it wouldn't hurt for Zoe to go to church, learn some Bible stories and some good manners to go with it. Early in October, a nice lady who was a regular customer at the diner invited Mary to go to church with her. Mary politely said she'd think about it, but something about the woman's invitation hit home. She reminded Mary of her nice neighbor from years ago, Mrs. Faust, who reached out to her when she was a little girl.

Just before Halloween, Mary started dropping Zoe off at Sunday School at the Methodist Church. Zoe asked her to come, but Mary always had an excuse. She had laundry to do, or had to get some shopping done. She'd get back to the church to pick Zoe up at noon, then they'd go to Waffle House for French toast and scrambled eggs. It was their special time together. Mary felt good about taking Zoe to church. She was proud that at her age, Zoe had already learned several Bible verses. Every Sunday at lunch she would quote and retell in dramatic detail the stories she had learned.

Zoe came home from church the Sunday before Thanksgiving more excited than usual. She announced that she had been chosen to be Mary, the baby Jesus' mother, in the Christmas Pageant and everyone would be there to see her. She told her mother that she had to make sure to do two things. First, she had to sit still and not fidget when the angel appeared to her. Second, she was supposed to carry the baby, carefully – like it was real, even though it was only a doll. She was supposed to use both arms and hold the baby like this, and not pick the baby up by one arm or just one leg. She was to act like a real mother.

Zoe had one line and she made Mary go over it every day for three weeks. She practiced it often and she practiced it loud. Mary asked why she had to be so loud. Zoe explained, with a whiff of condescension, that the "person in the back row" needed to hear. She then asked her mother if she knew who that person in the back row was.

Her one line was to come after the angel Gabriel announced that she was going to have a baby who would be the Son of God – and then she was to say, "May it be to me just as you have said."

Zoe asked Mary if she would finally, please, please come to church with her. Mary had managed to avoid going up to now. She didn't tell Zoe, but inside she didn't feel right being in a church. She felt like a failure, like everyone was judging her. But deeper than that, she felt like she was disqualified from life, like she'd failed God. The last thing she wanted was to be in a place that would remind her of everything that was wrong with her life. But her daughter in the Christmas pageant was different. "I wouldn't miss it for the world," she assured Zoe.

Sunday night couldn't come soon enough. The program was to start at 6:00 and Zoe had to be at the church at 4:45. Mary dropped her off and drove around for a while, got some gas in the car, and had a smoke.

She planned her entrance, figuring it would be better not to come in too early, but also not walk in late. She parked the car, took a deep breath, then slipped in the side door that entered the sanctuary to the right of the organ, near the front. She quickly found a seat in the third row, relieved that no one had spoken to her.

The church was as lovely as she remembered it. The walls of the sanctuary were cream white with powder blue trim. The vaulted ceiling was stamped tin painted a soft shade of rose. The floor and pews were all oak. The place always smelled like Murphy's soap. Little had changed.

The church seated about 150 people and the heavy ornate pews curved around the front of the platform. The floor sloped gently down to the altar, just enough so that, if, say, during the offering, someone's change might spill out of their purse, the coins could roll all the way down to the front. This was why years ago, Mary always wanted to sit in the first or second row. One time a quarter rolled between her legs. She was quick enough to catch it, and made it home with the treasure without anyone suspecting a thing. The only other time something rolled her way turned out to be a mint lifesaver. She tried to get it, but it got away from her and dropped down the large iron floor register.

The sanctuary was lined with garland and tiny white lights. The organ was quietly playing sweet familiar carols. Mary remembered that she often sat for the opening of Sunday church in this very section. One time she was given a slowpoke sucker at the end of Sunday School for learning a Bible verse. She had carefully taken the wrapping off and got a few licks in before the service started when a grown-up made a face at her. She quickly stuck it under the pew. It was to the far right end of either the second or third row, she wasn't sure. She remembered going back to the same spot the next Sunday. She would unstick the Slowpoke and get a few more licks in before anyone saw her, then stick it back under the seat. This went on for several weeks.

She wondered if this was the same seat and also wondered if, just maybe, it might still be there. She reached down and back under her seat, then bent over, pretending she was getting something out of her purse. She reached under the seat in front of her, feeling around for it. Nope, it wasn't there. In her quest, however, she brushed the leg of the elderly man in front of her. He turned and smiled. She was so embarrassed. She just knew that everyone was staring at her.

The sanctuary slowly filled with people, and the memories came like a flood. She realized that the little church had actually been a happy place for her, one of the few happy places in her life. The feeling of the memory surprised her. She remembered that Sunday School started at 9:45 downstairs. They met around splintery old round plywood tables in musty cramped classrooms that lined each side of a long hallway. All the children would then go upstairs at 11:00 for the first part of big church with the grownups. After the offering, they were escorted back downstairs for children's church, which happened in the main fellowship hall under the sanctuary.

Children's church was led by a nice lady, Mrs. Campbell, and her son. They told Bible stories with characters painted on flannel that stuck like magic on a large board. Mary remembered the stories as being wonderful. She would frantically raise her hand in hopes of being picked to place a flannel piece on the board – a cloud, or a tree, a sheep, or maybe a story character.

Mrs. Campbell played the piano every Sunday for children's church. All the children called her Grandma Campbell. Mary wished she really was her grandma. She was an older lady, and a rather large one. Mary remembered watching Grandma Campbell sit at the piano, facing away from the children as they sang. Her round body all but covered a small rickety piano bench.

Mary recalled her fascination watching that bench creak and sway back and forth as Grandma Campbell played. She watched intently just in case it might collapse under the strain. She remembered feeling guilty almost wishing it would happen just once, but it never did.

Grandma Campbell played with lots of energy, stretching her hands out to both ends of the piano, and then pulling them back in again – back and forth, in and out, up and down. Her body bounced along with it. She usually wore long sleeves, but sometimes they came down just halfway, and the rolls of fat that hung down over her elbows would bob back and forth as she played, keeping perfect time. It was mesmerizing.

Grandma wore thick glasses, and Mary was sure she had eyes or maybe a little camera hidden in the bun of her hair in the back of her head. She always knew immediately if a boy or girl was whispering or misbehaving during the singing. Grandma would stop playing, look straight up without turning around, and call a child by name, then gently say: "Now, Edwin, we're singing to Jesus and he loves when we sing to him, so let's do our best and not whisper!"

After children's church, Grandma Campbell would hug any child who would hang around - anybody who wanted one. Mary remembered the first time she got a hug from her. The woman was not much over five feet tall. She would turn towards you, clap her hands once and look you in the eye. Her face would erupt in an explosion of joy and surprise, calling your name like you were her only child who lived far away and you'd just surprised her for Christmas. Behind her thick glasses her kind brown eyes were the size of saucers. "That's the way love looks," Mary thought.

Grandma would take Mary's face between her soft hands and study her for just a second, then close her eyes and slowly pull her towards her. She would take a child completely into her big soft body. You could get lost in there. Mary so much wanted to get lost in Grandma's loving embrace. You could smell her perfume and the powder on her cheeks. And then she'd whisper your name in your ear, followed by the same words every Sunday. "You are such a special child." Mary would quietly stand near Grandma Campbell as she gave her hugs, hoping she could get one too. Grandma never failed her.

Why was she remembering all this?

The lights went down and Mary snapped out of her dream. The program started with a greeting from the pastor, a younger man. They sang a carol, some handbells played, and then a young teenage boy came up and played a drum solo. The program said the song was "Little Drummer Boy," but you had to imagine it because there was no melody - just a snare drum. There were a couple announcements, an offering, and then the pageant began.

The children were darling, and despite the request not to do so, some parents snuck up the aisle to take pictures. Then it was finally time for Zoe to come out. She waltzed out and on to the stage, magnificent in her blue robe as the mother Mary. She was radiant and she beamed the widest smile as the angel appeared. He was a tall gangly boy who struggled to remember his lines as he announced that Mary would have a baby and that she would be overcome by the Holy Spirit so that the child to be born would be called the Son of God. He was to be given the name, Jesus, because he would save his people from their sins.

Zoe slowly nodded her head as if to keep time until the precise moment for her one line. Mary leaned forward and mouthed the words with her daughter, channeling every syllable across the room. Zoe didn't need the help. She stood up straight, projected all the way to the back row, and announced with slow, punctuated words – "May-it-be-to-me-just-as-you-have-said."

The scene changed to the shepherds in the fields, the angels' song, and then to the manger. Zoe appeared again, sitting on a small stool at the manger. As the children sang "Away in a Manger," Zoe carefully lifted the baby Jesus out of the manger and cradled the doll gently in her arms. Mary fought back tears as the children sang. The words floated up from her heart. She was surprised how she remembered them.

> *Be near me Lord Jesus, I ask Thee to stay,*
> *Close by me forever and love me I pray.*
> *Bless all the dear children in Thy tender care,*
> *And fit us for heaven to live with Thee there.*

Zoe was simply elegant as the baby's mother, and it was all so beautiful - until the shepherds jumped up from their positions after the song and one of their staffs bopped poor Joseph on the head. He seemed O.K. though. Then everyone stood and they all sang "Silent Night" while lighting the candles that were passed out with the programs. Warm candlelight spread across the sanctuary. It was magical.

Mary's heart pounded as she sang. The words drew her in. She'd never really paid attention to them. They enveloped her like a warm hug - surrounding her, behind her, above her, beneath her.

Silent Night, Holy Night,
Son of God, love's pure light.
Radiant beams from Thy Holy face,
With the dawn of redeeming grace.
Jesus, Lord at Thy birth.
Jesus, Lord at Thy birth.

Mary felt strangely clean, and she didn't want it to end.

The lights came up, and the program was over. Mary stood and began to make her way across the sanctuary to the exit at the opposite side door, still hoping no one would speak to her.

That is when she spotted her. A little old lady with a walker was being helped out of her pew by a younger woman. It took only a moment for Mary to recognize her. It was Grandma Campbell. She shuffled slowly out of her row, with her head bent low. She looked so small, so frail. Mary paused in the aisle to let the women out when Grandma Campbell stopped, slowly angled her head upward to get a good look, and their eyes locked. She studied Mary's face for several seconds.

She wore the same thick glasses, but the eyes were not as bright. The woman's sight was weak, but she could see well enough. She stood there, scanning past Mary's eyes, looking deep into her soul. She then slowly took her hands off her walker and stretched out her arms. Mary leaned forward as the old woman took her face in both hands. Grandma traced Mary's profile with her soft touch, brushing her hair, rubbing her cheeks. She held her there for several seconds. She then pulled her close, pressed her cheek to Mary's, then tenderly whispered one word in her ear, "Child". She pulled back and smiled, holding Mary's face for another second. She then let her go, turned, and slowly continued up the aisle.

Mary was shaking. She felt like all the air had gone out of her, or maybe life itself had just flowed into her.

She gathered herself, turned and made her way to the side door just as Zoe came running up the stairs. "Mommy! Mommy! Did you see me? Did you see? "Was I as good a Mary as you?"

"You were SUPERTREMENDIFICENT!" Mary giggled and hugged her tight. They got in the car and Zoe dramatically recounted every nuance of the play. When they got home, they changed into their pajamas, ate pancakes, brushed teeth, and then Mary crawled into bed with Zoe. They laid on their backs and whispered in the dark. Zoe again walked Mary through the whole play. They stared up at the ceiling and recited the lines together and giggled.

Mary hugged Zoe tight and told her how proud she was of her. She then began to tell her stories of when she was a little girl, going to that same church. She told her of the memories of Sunday School, the flannelgraph Bible stories, the coins rolling across the floor, the slow poke sucker, and how she saw Grandma Campbell again tonight and how wonderful it was to be back there.

Zoe was quiet. Mary turned to her little girl and saw she was fast asleep. She stroked Zoe's hair, then the Mother Mary gently kissed the little Mary on the cheek, slid out of bed, tucked the covers in, then tiptoed out of the room.

She went across the hallway to her own room and turned off the light. Mary laid on top of the bed, her blue robe still wrapped tight around her. She remained there for the longest time, her mind retrieving memories of years past – her childhood, the baby she gave away, thoughts about God, thoughts about love. Could there still be love for her? Could God still be there? Would God still want her? After all she'd done? After all she'd failed to do? Could there still be hope for her? She turned her glance towards the window with the shades open to the night sky. The stars were clear and bright.

She remembered the words. "The Holy Spirit shall come upon you and the power of the Most High shall overshadow you."

As she lay there, warm tears surfaced from deep wells, bubbling up from years of pent up longing – as she whispered the words again, softly, like a prayer that was always there, waiting to be offered up again for the very first time.

"May it be to me just as you have said."

Rocky
Christmas Eve 2014

The sign read, Dr. Robert D. Livingwood. It had hung in that same place on that same office door for seven years, but he stopped to look at it anyway. Maybe it would help him regain his bearings, find his identity again. He felt he was losing track of who he was.

Robert Livingwood was not yet thirty-eight years old, but he was nearing the top of his profession. He was a neonatal cardio-thoracic surgeon. He was teaching, doing research, and practicing surgery at the University Hospital. He was making his mark in the world. He was published and was fielding a steady stream of invitations to present at medical conferences around the country. His research on genetic fetal heart abnormalities and breakthrough diagnostic techniques were gaining notice.

Life had sped up for him, and the demands were growing by the day. He had little time for anything, and certainly no time for love. He had just purchased a small condo a half mile from the hospital. His life was moving along nicely, until July when his father died suddenly of a stroke.

Robert was an only child. His parents married late an had him when they were forty. His mother, Irma Jean was now seventy-eight. She also had a weak heart. She'd had several stents put in over the years. Now on top of all that she was showing signs of dementia. Robert was watching her closely, squeezing in the ninety mile trip back home to check on her every week, sometimes twice a week.

With each visit, he could tell she was slipping a bit more. Perhaps it was her age, or partly due to grief. Either way, he knew the day was coming when he'd have to do something. She was forgetting important things and remembering not so important things. She forgot to feed her cat, but would change the kitty litter several times a day. It was a clean cat.

It all came to a head Monday morning, the first of December. He got a call from the police department in his hometown. His mother had gone outside early in the morning to take out the trash but then had closed the door behind her, locking her outside. It was a cold morning, and she was in her bathrobe and slippers.

She wandered around to the back of the house, then started down the street knocking on doors. Most neighbors had gone to work. Those who hadn't were still sleeping. She walked north three blocks and then forgot why she was out there.

Just about then the garbage man drove by and recognized her, picked her up and took her back to the house. He called the police. They got a locksmith, got her back inside, and found Robert's phone number in big red letters on a sticky note on the fridge. He had put it there just that previous Friday.

That pretty much did it for him. The next afternoon he started looking for assisted living facilities near his home. He found a good one, and they had an opening, but it wouldn't be ready until after the new year. What should he do? He couldn't leave her there. He tried to see if a cousin or a neighbor could stay with her for a few weeks, but the holidays were coming, and no one was available to help.

He didn't have a choice. He had to move her in with him. He dreaded the thought of it, but he didn't know what else to do. His schedule leading up to Christmas was packed full. He'd just have to do the best he could. Irma Jean had days where you couldn't tell anything was wrong, and then there'd be times where she didn't know what time it was.

Life was changing for her too, but one thing that hadn't changed was how efficient she was at making him feel guilty. Robert could feel guilty all on his own without anyone else's help, but she could make him feel terrible. He went to get her, loaded up some of her things and brought her to his place.

On the drive home, she talked constantly. "You don't need to worry about me. I'll just be in the way. You have your work. I know I'm just a bother. I wish God would get it over with and take me. Then you wouldn't have to worry about me. I'd be gone and you'd be free to live your life. I doubt you'd even be sad if I died. I think you'd actually be glad to see me go."

She'd ramble on like that for quite a while, then when he couldn't take any more, he would interrupt her and say, "Mother, don't talk like that. You're my mother. Of course, I'd be sad if anything happened to you. You're not in the way. You're my mother."

She'd sit quiet for a while, and then start the same conversation all over again.

That's what Robert said, but it wasn't how he felt. She was right, in a way. She *was* holding him back. Every time he thought he might be able to carve out some time for his research, something would happen and he'd have to run and tend to her. His career was about to take off, and she was a lead weight pulling him back to the runway.

Opportunities were opening up for him. He felt he was on the brink of doing something significant, making his mark on the world. But here he was having to take care of one old woman.

He felt guilty for feeling that way. He was driven to succeed as far back as he could remember. He finished high school early and graduated from college summa cum laude when he was nineteen. He entered medical school and finished his residency before he turned twenty-four.

As he stood there, looking at the nameplate on his office door, he imagined the day when a medical procedure would be named after him. There would be an oil portrait of him displayed along the main corridor of the hospital. Fifty years from now, doctors around the world would be consulting with each other over the most difficult cases. "What treatment did you use on that patient? What a remarkable recovery! How did you do it?" And they would say, "We did the 'Livingwood Procedure', and he pulled through." They would speak in reverent tones and everyone would nod knowingly.

Thousands of people would be alive because of him. Sick babies would survive and grow to become school teachers, inventors, senators, or astronauts. Adult survivors from around the world would write him letters, thanking him for saving their lives.

He would prove his father wrong.

Throughout his childhood and early adult years, his father had hardly noticed him. Never once did he tell Robert he had done good, that he was proud of him. Then last summer he suffered a massive stroke and was gone. His father was a tool and die maker, and Robert sometimes wondered if he felt his life didn't amount to much compared to his son's accomplishments.

Robert was sure his father was proud of him. He just never told him. The closest thing his father ever said to acknowledge his medical work was when his mother would call and ask him to do something for them. Robert would have to tell them that he'd get to it later because his schedule was too full. When he finally did get home to visit, he'd walk in the door and his father would hardly look at him. He'd right walk past him, and then say with a touch of sarcasm, "Dr Livingwood I presume." Robert hated that. He heard it all the time in his early years of medical school.

It was Friday, the week before Christmas. Robert was making rounds with an entourage of medical students when a call came. It was the trauma line at the ER. Someone had brought in an infant with a heart issue. He thought it would be a good teaching moment, so he took the group down with him.

They entered the triage room to find a newborn. It was a boy, a preemie. "I'm guessing thirty-five, thirty-six weeks," surmised the ER doctor. The baby was wrapped in a warming blanket and placed in an isolette with IV's for fluids. "Where are it's parents?" Robert asked. "There are no parents," the nurse said. "They brought him from the Bismarck hotel. A housekeeper found him early this morning – somebody wrapped him in bedsheets and placed him in a laundry bin. He must have been born sometime during the night. The umbilical cord was still attached."

"How's he doing?"

"Well, he's a tough little guy. In pretty good shape for having such a rough start. A little dehydrated. Luckily it was warm in there and he was wrapped up."

A police officer standing off in the corner of the room spoke up. "The housekeeper said she went to get a load of laundry and felt a lump and heard a faint whimper. She called 911 and they brought him here. Lucky she was paying attention. He would have ended up in the wash for sure."

"Why'd you call me?" Robert asked as he bent over the child. The ER doc said, "Well, it is an unusual case, and, besides, we think he might have an ASD (atrial septal defect)."

Robert already knew. He could hear the familiar swishing sound caused by a hole in the heart chamber as he pressed his stethoscope to the baby's tiny chest. He studied the child. He was about the right size for thirty-five weeks. His complexion was shriveled and ruddy, with a touch of jaundice, and he was trying with all his strength to muster a cry.

"A laundry bin!" What in the world!" Robert said to no one in particular. The Bismarck was near downtown, an old dive of a hotel. Homeless people and addicts stayed there. It was known for some seedy activity. It had quite a reputation.

As Robert listened to the heart, one of the female students turned abruptly and walked out of the room. "Where's Chaney going?" Robert snapped. "Give her a minute sir," another student said. "What's wrong?" Robert asked as he looked to the door.

"I think it just kind of got to her. She'll be O.K."

"Well, if she wants to be a doctor, she'd better be." he snapped while still listening to the heart.

"Sir, I think it's because she's adopted."

Robert looked up at the student, then glanced at the others, paused, then went back to the baby. He gathered himself and had each student listen to the heart.

"It got to her," he thought. Well, it kind of got to him too. Life is more than unfair. It can be downright cruel. And what an unlikely chain of events that they found him alive.

He checked in on the child throughout the day and again on Saturday. Robert agreed with the NICU team that the heart issue, though it would have to be addressed eventually, could wait. The boy needed to stabilize and gain some weight.

He was a tough little guy. Robert named him Rocky. He handwrote the name on the boy's ID card. Very unprofessional.

His thoughts kept coming back to the boy throughout the day. "Who was his mother? Where was she? Was she safe? And why would she leave him in a laundry bin? Did she hope he would die? Or did she hope he would survive?" Sometimes life is simply a mystery.

That Sunday night he had to fly to Boston to speak at a day-long medical conference. He returned home late Monday night. He paid a neighbor's older teenage daughter to stay with his mother. He got home, slept for three hours then was up again to prepare a research proposal abstract to present to a Dr. Jonas Ianarra, the head neonatal cardiologist at Johns Hopkins. He scrubbed for surgery at 7 a.m., then delivered a lecture, then he took the rest of the afternoon to write. He stopped by the NICU to check on the baby. Little Rocky seemed to be doing well. That was good.

By the time Robert was done for the day, it was dark and raining hard. A thick fog had set in. He hadn't seen his mother in nearly forty-eight hours, and he hadn't had much sleep. He got in his car to head home.

Up ahead about a block, through the rain and fog, he recognized the familiar shape of an ambulance. He didn't pay much attention to it until he noticed that it turned into his neighborhood. His heart skipped, then started to pound when the truck turned on to his street. Every frightful thought rushed through his head. "Oh no, what if it's mother. I haven't been there for her. I've neglected her, now she's gone and done something or her heart has given out and I wasn't there."

His worst fears came to fruition as he watched the truck turn into his driveway. He pulled in behind it. He could hardly see for the rain.

A man in a uniform jumped out, ran to the back, and pulled open the door. Robert was out in a flash. "I'm a doctor," he said. "Can I help?" The man was digging something out of the back of the truck. He leaned out in the rain, looked at him, paused, then said, "O.K." He turned around quickly, reached in and handed Robert a stack of cold flat cardboard boxes.

They were frozen TV dinners.

It was a Schwann's truck.

Robert looked up and saw Irma Jean standing at the front door in her bathrobe. He ran up the steps with the stack of TV dinners. She had ordered three dozen of them. Every one of them was Salisbury steak, mashed potatoes and gravy, peas, and carrots.

She opened the door. He rushed in and set the trays on the table. "Good Lord, mother, what are you doing?"

"What are you doing is what I want to know," she said. "Look at you! You're not eating. You're not sleeping! If you're not going to take care of yourself, someone else is going to have to do it. It's a good thing I moved in. You won't make it without me!"

He looked at her, then went back outside to pay the driver. He rushed back inside, found room in the freezer for all the TV dinners, dried off, then poured himself a cup of coffee and sat down with Irma Jean at the kitchen table.

"Mother, I really appreciate you looking out for me. But I'm really fine. You don't have to worry about me. But thank you just the same. I am so sorry I haven't been home much these past few days. You gave me a scare."

"Well, you scare me sometimes." She said. "You're all I've got. Sometimes I don't think I know you." Then she softened, and wrapped her thin hands over his as he cradled his coffee. "You know there's nothing I wouldn't do for you, Bobby."

He cleared his throat. "And there's nothing I wouldn't do for you either, Momma."

"Good," she said as she straightened up and slapped his hand. "I was expecting you'd say that, because tomorrow's Christmas Eve, and it would mean everything to me for you to drive me back home and take me to the carol service at the church. It starts at 6:00."

"Oh, mother," Robert tilted his head in feigned sympathy. "I'm sorry. I have a full day tomorrow. To top it off, there's a reception at 4:00 at the University Club. It's for the chief neonatal cardiologist from Johns Hopkins. I've been working all week on an abstract proposal to present to him. If I can get him to agree to collaborate with me on some research, I could have my name published next to his. It would open so many doors. I've got to meet with him, mother. I've got to go to that reception."

"Oh Bobby. All those people are peacocks. They're just going to strut around, talk loud, and eat cheese."

"Mother, this is important."

"Oh," she paused. "I know it is honey." She looked away. "You're right. You go ahead. I'll just sit here at home. I don't want to be in your way. I'll be O.K. Don't worry about me. There will be other Christmases."

She got up, set her coffee cup in the sink, kissed him on the forehead and went to bed.

"Ohhh!" He felt such guilt. A meeting with Dr. Ianella could catapult his career. An opportunity like this might never come again. Then again, this could be his mother's last Christmas, or at least the last one that she'll ever remember.

He was exhausted, but he tossed and turned all night. He hated himself if he did and hated himself if he didn't. The next morning he knew what he had to do.

He came into the kitchen. Irma Jean was standing at the sink pouring water into the tea kettle. He snuck up behind her and kissed her on the cheek. "Momma, you're right. I'll drive you home this evening and we'll go to church together." She turned, looked into his eyes, smiled sweetly, then took his face in her soft, paper thin hands. "Oh, you're so precious. It will be just wonderful!"

He worked until 3:30, then called her to make sure she was ready. He hurried back to the condo to pick her up, and they headed out for the drive back home to go to the Christmas Eve service at the Second Presbyterian church.

They arrived about ten minutes early. They had stopped for a sandwich and coffee to go. Robert needed it. He hadn't slept in days. They sat in the third row on the left, the same row they occupied as a family when he was a boy. There were hugs from several older ladies who remembered him. At 6:00, there were about fifty people present, most of them older, with a handful of kids who were there to be in the program.

The service started with a carol. The piano player couldn't see or hear the notes, and she held the sustain pedal down the entire song. It was terrible, but they all got through it. Robert fought sleep the whole time, his mind buzzing in a fog somewhere between the hard pew he was sitting in and the reception along with the future that he was missing back at the University Club.

Mary and Joseph came out on the stage, wearing bathrobes. The baby Jesus was a plastic doll. Then there were shepherds abiding in the fields, watching their flocks by night. Suddenly an angel came upon them, and the glory of the Lord shone round about them, and they were sore afraid.

Robert tried to listen as his eyelids drooped. Thankfully the lights were turned down low so nobody noticed his head bobbing.

And the angel said unto them, "Fear not, for I bring you good tidings of great joy, which shall be for all people." The ancient words were familiar to him, and took him back to his childhood. "For unto you is born this day in the city of David, a Savior, which is Christ the Lord."

Though his eyes grew heavy, the words were warm and comforting, beckoning from a forgotten place from long ago. His eyes closed, and the angel's voice went on, fading into the distance.

"And this will be a sign unto you, you shall find the baby . . . you shall find the baby . . .wrapped in bed sheets, and lying in a laundry bin."

Robert's eyes snapped open and he sat straight up. The angel was a tall girl, and she kept saying her lines as if nothing was out of sorts. Did he just hear what he thought he heard? He looked over at his mother. She was smiling. No one else seemed to be thrown off by anything out of the ordinary.

"You shall find the baby wrapped in bed sheets and lying in a laundry bin." The words reverberated through his head. The service continued, but he was somewhere else, lost in thought. A laundry bin, in a moldy rundown flea-bitten hotel. "You shall find the baby - poor, weak, and vulnerable among the homeless, the seedy, the broken. That's where you'll find the child. That's where the Christ will be."

Robert was stunned by the thought. Was a dirty manger in a drafty old barn any different than this? Did the Creator of the galaxies, black holes, tectonic plates, DNA strands, and atrial nerves really leave all that majesty behind to come to earth as a homeless baby?

The service ended. They said their goodbyes then started home.

About thirty minutes down the road, Robert had to ask. "Did you sense anything different about that play tonight, Mother?" Irma Jean just smiled, dreaming out the window. She turned to him. "It was wonderful. Weren't those children precious?"

Robert stared at the road. She must not have heard anything. Was he just dreaming? Was he the crazy one? Maybe he was the one with dementia.

They got home and he helped his mother get to bed, but he couldn't sleep. He poured a cup of coffee, and was ready to sit down on the couch, but then couldn't help himself. He jumped up, got his coat on, hopped in the car and headed for the hospital.

He made his way to the NICU. A young doctor sauntered down the hall, and surprised to see him that late at night, greeted him, "Dr. Livingwood, I presume!"

Robert just glared at him and kept on walking, down the right corridor, through the double doors and then to room nine where Rocky was.

The attending nurse was just coming out of the room. "Hello? Doctor?" She too was surprised to see him there that late, and on Christmas Eve.

"How's our boy doing?"

She stopped and managed a weary smile. "He's had a pretty good day. He's gained another ounce. Is there anything I can do for you?" Robert shook his head. She turned and continued down the hall.

Robert went in quietly, removed his coat, and pulled a stool up to the side of the isolette. He was going to snap on some gloves, but reached for the sanitizer instead. He slipped his right hand through the opening in the side and arranged a couple of the lead wires. "How are we doing old boy? You're a tough one, you are."

The lights were low. The steady beep of the heart monitor had a soothing effect on him. The boy's vitals were good, but the heart showed the recognizable slight abnormality on the graph.

Robert stroked the child's head, then stretched out his little finger and slipped it into Rocky's tiny hand. The baby grasped it and held on tight.

Robert sat there quietly, for the longest time, watching the baby, his little chest rising and falling softly as he breathed. Robert didn't move. Why was he a doctor anyway? Was it to be important? To make a name for himself? Or was it for moments like this?

"What's going to come of you little man?" he asked as he gently rubbed the palm of the boy's tiny hand.

Somewhere back in Sunday School, Robert remembered something Jesus said about "the least of these." No one could be more "least" than this little one with no mother, no family, abandoned in a hotel laundry bin, and fighting for his life.

"There must be a reason," Robert thought. How else could anyone explain how the boy was found and how he ended up here. Perhaps he's destined for greatness. Maybe it's all part of a plan. Maybe he'll be a poet, or an inventor, a politician, or maybe a surgeon. Maybe he'll be a healer of hearts. Maybe he'll change the world.

Wrapped in bedsheets and lying in a laundry bin. Robert couldn't get his mind around it - someone so small with the potential to become something so big. And then he thought about the story from earlier that night, about Jesus' own birth - someone so big, becoming something so small. Was there some kind of cosmic connection to it all?

Robert glanced up at the clock on the wall just as the minute hand struck midnight, and he remembered the time.

It was Christmas once again.

Beings of Unbearable Light
Christmas Eve, 2015

It has been a warm and wet week at the Milford farm, warmer than usual. Last Friday it rained hard all night and on through the next afternoon. Old farmer Milford spent the entire Saturday working in the barn, cleaning the mud out of the stalls, putting down fresh straw. He fed all the animals, cleaned out the water trough, then filled it with fresh water. He finished just as the sun was going down, gave everything a final look, turned out the lights, grabbed his umbrella, and headed back to the house. The barn went dark, except for a random distant spark of lightning flashing through the cracks in the barn siding. So out of place for December.

The animals were all parked in their stalls. They weren't tired. After all, it was still early. There were Orville and Wilbur, the work horses. They were brothers, of course. Then there were B-e-e-e-n-n-n-n and B-o-o-o-n-n-n-n-i-e, the lambs. There was Thumbelina the cow, Henrietta and Marletta the chickens. Up in the rafters was Zoe the mourning dove, and then there was Mort, the pig. Mort was the spokesman of the group.

They all lay there, whispering to each other in the dark, telling jokes.

Then someone called over to Mort who was lounging in the last stall on the left. "Mort, tell us a story."

"Oh, I'm getting old. I don't know if I can remember any stories," he grunted.

"Yes, you do. We know you do. Tell us a story."

Then someone cried out, "Tell us the story of the Boy Child!"

Mort paused, "I think I just told that one a couple years ago. How about I tell a different one?" He thought for a second, then asked, "Have you ever heard the story about the Beings of Unbearable Light?"

They looked at each other. None of them had ever heard of that one.

"Well, alright then," he said.

He waddled out of his stall, and ambled towards the center of the barn where the old John Deere was parked. He climbed up on the tractor and plopped on the seat. He spun around backwards, leaned against the steering wheel, and crossed one leg over the other. You know, the way pigs do.

Mort began:

It was a long time ago, far away in the heavenlies. Two beings - two mid-level Beings of Unbearable Light were summoned to the throne.

(I have to stop and explain something to you, the reader. The phrase, 'Beings of Unbearable Light' is the name that the animals have for what we would call 'angels.' Now we don't see angels very often. Our eyes are too dim. And if we were to see them, we would likely not recognize them because our hearts are too hard. Animals, however, see them quite often. But even when they do see one, it still catches them by surprise. When they happen to see an angel, they just shake.

Perhaps you have observed this. A dog will be lying down, get up, turn and go to another room and then just stop for a second and shudder. Horses do this too. You wouldn't have known it, but likely they've seen an angel.)

Mort continued:

Two Beings of Unbearable Light were summoned to the throne. One of their names was spelled 'A-a-r-k and the other's name was spelled 'A-a-r-o-l-d. You would think their names were pronounced "Aark" and "Aarold", but the little backwards apostrophe preceding the name, which appears in some ancient languages, indicates what is called a 'glottal fricative.' All this means is that a word with a glottal fricative begins with a hard "H" sound. Their names were spelled that way, but were really pronounced this way: "Haark" and "Haarold."

Two Beings of Unbearable Light were summoned to the throne. Now Haarold was a scriptwriter. He was a master of language. He was good at breaking things down and keeping everything quite simple. He was often called on to write out scripts for heralds who would go and deliver a message to the mortal world.

Haarold had been busy a few months earlier, preparing the script for the archangel Gabriel, who was sent to a young virgin girl to tell her that she was going to bear the child of the Almighty. Haarold then had to write a second script to send with Gabriel to take to the girl's fiancé to kind of set things straight.

Haark, on the other hand, was a master musician. He had composed thousands of anthems for the throne.

Haarold and Haark reported immediately. The Elder behind the desk welcomed them. They could hardly mask their excitement over being called. All of the angels knew that the Fulfillment of the Ages was coming. All of heaven was electric with excitement. Haarold and Haark had been hoping that maybe, just maybe, they would be asked to have a part in it.

The Elder pulled out a folder, opened it, and reviewed the notes on a piece of parchment as he said to them, "We have assignments for you." He turned first to Haarold. "Haarold, you are to write the script to bring the message of the Christ child's birth to the mortals. You have to be brief and you have to be simple in your language, because, as you know, as precious as they are, the mortals are rather limited."

"There's quite a bit of content here." He pulled a second sheet of paper from the folder. He flashed it in front of Haarold in one hand, and slapped it emphatically with the back of his other hand.

"You have to include all of it. It's all got to be there."

"First," he said, returning his glance to the paper, "You have to - as we always have to do, and you know this - the messenger has to assure them that they don't need to be afraid. This is because, as you know very well, before any one of us gets a word out, the mortals will be paralyzed with fear. Their faces will be planted in the ground."

"After they gain their composure, they need to know that this is good news for the entire world, not just for their kind."

"Then, they need to know that the child to be born is descended from the royal but mortal line of David."

"The fourth thing you have to convey is that this child is the long-awaited Anointed One who will bring salvation to the world."

"And finally, they need to know the child's Name. His is the matchless Name which stands above every other. They need to know what we all know, that the child existed before time. And He will stand at the end of time. He is Lord of all."

"Oh, and another thing." The Elder rechecked the paper. "They need to know where to find the child. And then they'll need a sign to help them know that they've found the right one."

"Got that?"

Haarold was writing feverishly. As he scanned his scribbled notes, he pressed his lips together, tilted his head to the side, and said, "You ask much!"

The Elder laughed and said, "No, we're asking you."

Then the Elder turned to Haark. "Now Haark, because words are never sufficient, you are to write a song to follow up the message so the mortals will be sure to get it.

Haark gushed, "Well you're bowling right up my alley.

What kind of song do you want?" The Elder pressed both hands together to his lips and said thoughtfully, "It has to be a song that brings the heavenlies together with the fallen world, because that alone is worthy of the Name. You must capture it in some way."

Haark's creative juices were already flowing. He thought, "Something this important warrants a big choir." He gathered up the courage to make a bold request. He asked, "Can it be arranged for a full Division to be given for the choir?"

(Now I need to tell you another thing. A "Division" in heavenly terms consists of ten thousand Beings of Unbearable Light. That's a tremendously large choir.)

The Elder slapped the desk, reared back and laughed. Then he jumped up and came around and stood between Haark and Haarold. He turned them outward, and put both his arms around their shoulders, as if to point them to some imaginary scene. They weren't sure what.

With the flamboyance of a film director, the Elder gave a broad gesture and said, "No, we're going bigger than that. It won't be one Division. It will be ten thousand Divisions!"

Haark did the calculations in his head. Ten thousand Divisions, or ten thousand times ten thousand would equal one hundred million! One hundred million Beings of Unbearable Light would come crashing down on a dark and fallen world!

Haark's heart pounded. He gathered his composure to ask the next question. The Elder was leaning forward, hands on his knees, nodding his head with an open-mouthed smile as if he was anticipating it. "Yes! Go ahead, ask!"

Haark cleared his throat. "And who is the audience?"

The Elder jumped up and clapped his hands in delight. "Hah! That's the thing! The audience will be five old guys in a field!"

Haark gasped. "One hundred million Beings of Unbearable Light would overwhelm the physical universe. How in the world would only five old guys in a field see it?"

By the time Haark got his question out, the Elder was already walking away. "Oh, we've figured that out too! No one else is going to see it. Only those five guys!"

He turned and kept on walking, laughed and threw his hands in the air. "Oh Elohim! What a sense of humor!" "The joke," he announced as he emphatically shook his index finger in the air, "is on them!"

Haark and Haarold looked at each other. They knew immediately who the "them" were. "Them" were the principalities and dark powers of the heavenly realms that had enslaved the mortal world.

Before the Elder disappeared out of sight, Haarold called out one more question. "One hundred million Beings of Unbearable Light! Would there be room for us to come along too?"

Without turning around, the Elder gave a quick wave of the hand, and yelled, "Of course! What's two more!" And he disappeared laughing all the way.

Haark and Haarold looked at each other and said, "We'd better get busy!" So they went back and got to work.

Haarold started on the text. The appointed messenger was one of the archangels named Raphael, whose name means "God heals." Haarold finished his script in a matter of hours.

Haark's assignment took a bit more time. As he worked, he could sense the creative power of the Almighty speaking into and spurring and clarifying his imagination. He was captivated by the thought of a choir so big. He had always written anthems for the throne. He had never written one for the mortal world to hear. For something so important, so big, he wanted a melody that was powerful and decisive. At the same time he wanted to arrange it in counterpoint, where legions of angels would call out a theme, and across the other horizon, more legions of angels would answer. The entire sky would erupt in explosions of joyful sound.

In time, the score was done. Then there were the rehearsals. "One hundred million voices!" he thought. "That's a lot of sheet music!"

Soon all was ready. The time came for the child to be born. It was like the day before D-Day. One hundred million and two Beings of Unbearable Light descended to earth undercover, ever so quietly in the dark. They all took their places, final instructions were given, then they waited.

———————————

Now there were shepherds abiding in the fields, keeping watch over their flocks by night.

And suddenly, Raphael stood among them, and the glory of the Lord shone round about them with unbearable light. And, of course, before Raphael could say a word, the shepherds were hugging the ground on their faces in sheer terror, shading their eyes from the blinding light. Raphael reached down and touched each one gently on the shoulder and said:

"Do not be afraid, for I bring you good news of great joy, which shall be for all people. For unto you is born this day in the city of David, a Savior, which is Christ the Lord. And this will be a sign unto you. You will find the baby wrapped in swaddling clothes and lying in a manger."

And then, as suddenly as he came, Raphael was gone.

The shepherds were slow to move. They peeled their faces up off the dirt. Keeping their heads low, they looked around cautiously, trying to catch their breath. Their hearts were racing.

They held their positions for a minute or two. Then just when they thought it safe enough for them to sit up, the entire sky exploded with light. The shepherds were rocked backwards as wave after shock wave of sound overwhelmed them. The trees bent over double. The wind blew and dirt and leaves and grass and twigs all spiraled upward in a violent whirlwind.

Haark gave the cue and the choir erupted,

Glory to God in the highest

The melody rocketed back and forth across the brilliant sky. Legions beyond legions of Beings of Unbearable Light, called out to each other in concussions of joyful sound.

And on Earth peace, goodwill towards men
On whom His favor rests.

The whole thing lasted no more than a minute, only because the poor shepherds could not have handled any more. And then it was done. The sky went black and the wind died down.

The five men held tight to the ground for several minutes. You would have thought they were dead. Then one by one, they slowly raised their heads. Their faces were ashen, drained of blood from the shock. But you wouldn't be able to tell because they were caked with mud. Their noses and ears were plugged with grass, and their hair was wild with leaves and twigs. They slowly rose to their knees, then managed to stand up on wobbly legs. They looked at each other in amazement. Wide eyed, they slowly patted themselves, the top of their heads, their faces, arms, front and backside, then their legs. They were taking inventory to see if all their body parts were still attached. They counted heads. All were accounted for. No one was missing.

Then one of them finally caught his breath, looked over to the others, and said, "We've got to go."

"Go where?"

"We've got to go and see this thing."

And so they did. They left the sheep with the youngest one and off they went.

Haark and Haarold hung around for a minute to see them go, and then joined the rest as they returned to the heavenlies. The place was alive with excitement. Everyone was exuberant. One hundred million Beings of Unbearable Light returned to heaven, laughing and slapping each other on the back. "That was so awesome!"

The Elder worked his way through the crowd and found Haark and Haarold. He hugged them both. "Wonderful! It was just wonderful! Everything was perfect!"

And in that moment, Haark cleared his throat to ask the question that he had always wanted to ask, that he never had the confidence to ask, but now just had to know.

"Sir, can I ask just one more question?" The Elder smiled, "Certainly, what is it?"

Haark leaned forward slightly and pursed his lips with great concern, "All that trouble for only five of them. Will the shepherds be the only ones to hear? Will they be the only ones to know?"

The Elder smiled warmly and took Haark's face in his hands. He turned and did the same with Haarold. He then said thoughtfully, "Oh no. The Almighty has already set things in motion."

He was planning to tell them shortly, but figured now was as good a time as any. The Elder addressed each of them.

"Haarold, you have received the message of the Anointed One. From now on, you will continue to whisper that message into the hearts of all whom the Almighty has appointed – those who will bear the good news to the mortals in every language, place, and time."

And then he turned to Haark and put a hand on his shoulder. "Haark, you have received a song. And from now on, you will whisper inspiration to all whom the Almighty has appointed to tell the story in song to all people in every language."

"In other words," he said, "your work is just beginning."

And that is what they did.

Haark and Haarold went to work, and they are still working to this day.

Haarold was right there with Matthew, Mark, and Luke, and John, and Paul and Peter and James, from John Chrysostom to John Calvin, from Luther to Whitefield to

Ding Limei, Martin Luther King, and Billy Graham - all who have carried the message through the centuries.

And Haark was there with Palestrina and Bach, Handel and Berlioz, Rosetti and Ives, and Rutter and Wilcox. He's been there with them all.

Now, that's not to say it's all gone perfectly without a hitch. About 250 years ago, Haark was standing next to a composer named Charles Wesley. As Wesley worked, Haark whispered into his ear, "Haark *and* Haarold, the Angels Sing," but it just came out different. Something happened, and it just came out different.

But it doesn't matter. It has all turned out well enough. The quirks and twists that come with human finiteness are bound to happen. But it doesn't matter, because the glory of the Lord is being revealed, and all flesh will see it together.

———————————

"The end," said Mort.

He backed down off the tractor, dropped to the ground, and waddled towards his stall. The animals sat quietly. Then one of them said, "Mort, did that really happen? Is that true?"

Mort answered wistfully. "Every word. More true than I can make it. Every last word."

Frosty the Snowman
Christmas Eve 2017

Pringles' department store had been in the family for four generations. It had occupied the same location since 1946, in a declining neighborhood just outside the inner circle of downtown Nashville.

The store carried a bit of everything – toys, clothes, some hardware, knickknacks. Competition from the larger box stores was tough, but people loved the nostalgia of the place. It featured creaky old wood floors and open beams on both the first and second floor.

The place always smelled like fresh popcorn and roasted peanuts, which you could get back at the lunch counter with its vintage soda fountain. A World War II era model train wound its way around the store. The coffee was the best in town, and the floor clerks were actually helpful. At Christmas, everything was decorated exquisitely, with antique ornaments, garland, and live lighted trees.

The main attraction, however, was Frosty the Snowman. He was a mime who greeted people as they entered the front door. He was one of those street entertainers who could hold a pose for inordinate amounts of time without blinking. Whenever someone came up and dropped in a coin or a dollar bill, Frosty would jerk to life, open his eyes wide, and dance a little jig.

Frosty's real name was Leonard Collins. He was born and raised in southeastern Kentucky. After high school, he bounced around a few odd jobs, then in 1968 his number came up in the draft and he was sent to Viet Nam. After his discharge, he joined the circus. He worked with the elephants for a couple years, then was invited to try out for the clown team. It was there that he learned to be a mime. He got to be pretty good at it. That was also how he met Jeanette. She worked in makeup.

They fell in love and got married. Life was wonderful until a few years later, a routine outpatient surgery went sour. Infection set in and Jeanette died suddenly. The surgery took place on a Wednesday. Leonard took her home that afternoon. Two days later she was fighting for her life. They admitted her back into the hospital Friday evening. Leonard sat by her bed the whole night. The next morning, the infection had intensified. They rushed her to intensive care, she went into a coma, and by Monday she was gone.

She died on a Labor Day. That was 18 years ago. After it happened, Leonard grieved deeply for her. He spent much of the first month in bed, then decided she wouldn't want him to live that way.

He needed some kind of purpose in life, so he went out and found a full bodied, white fluffy onesie. It wasn't easy. He was 6'2' and tipping 280 lbs. He rummaged through a number of thrift stores around Nashville and found a pair of black boots, a green scarf, red mittens, a wide black plastic belt, and a black derby hat. Around Halloween, he bought a large black plastic kettle. He sewed black buttons on his suit and found a place that could fashion a long foam-fitted carrot nose. He ordered two of them. The noses cost as much as the entire costume.

Leonard pitched the idea to Mr. Pringle in early November. Mr. Pringle agreed to give Leonard the opportunity. "We'll try it out for a season and see how things go."

On Thanksgiving Day, Leonard shaved his head. Friday morning, he covered every exposed inch of skin with white makeup. He put on his snowman suit and derby hat and set up shop on the covered sidewalk, in front of the main door of the store.

He arrived around 1:00, set his kettle down, struck a pose and held it. At first, people ignored him, put their heads down, and rushed past him into the store. But then a child ventured close, circled, and then jumped away giggling. Another child walked up and did the same thing, then another. Soon adults would come near for a closer look. They'd stop six feet away (never closer) and study his eyes to see if he would blink. "Amazing," they would say to each other. "It's as if he isn't even breathing!" When someone would drop a quarter or a dollar bill into the kettle, Frosty's eyes would blink open, and he would come to life and dance. He never said a word. Real mimes don't talk. And few people spoke to him. What do you say to a frozen snowman?

If someone dropped in a bit more, say a $10 or a $20, he'd dance a little longer. Children were delighted. Unlike the adults, they were not shy. They would run up to him, touch his snowsuit, then jump away, squealing with delight tinged with fear as his eyes opened wide, his body went into convulsions and he danced for them.

It didn't take long for Leonard to become a fixture at the store. Families would come from great distances just to see Frosty the Snowman. The larger crowds didn't hurt Mr. Pringle's business either.

For eighteen years, Frosty's routine was always the same. From the day after Thanksgiving through Christmas Eve, he would come every day of the week, arriving around 1:00, and do his thing until dusk. Then he'd change out of his costume, take the money he'd collected and go into the store and buy food, clothes, and toys. He didn't own a car, but would load up a cart and walk the neighborhood, making deliveries according to a list he'd kept of folks who'd had a tough year.

After making his rounds, he'd go back to the store and buy a few more items for one last stop. He'd load up with mittens, wool hats, blankets, sandwiches and hot coffee, and sometimes a tarp or a warm coat. He'd wheel the cart out the front door, around to the back of the store, across the employee parking lot, through a hole in the fence, across a railroad track, and into the woods where a dozen or so homeless men lived.

Frosty would deliver the gifts, visit for a few minutes, then head home, only to do it all over again the next day. Sometimes he collected enough money to cover it all, but more often than not, he chipped in with some of his own.

Other than Mr. Pringle, no one knew Frosty's real name except Bessie Russell. She had worked at Pringles' since before Leonard first started. She would often help him with his shopping. After so many years, she had a good idea of the things he would want. Sometimes she had the cart ready for him when he came into the store.

Bessie had worked at Pringles' for twenty-seven years. She wanted to retire, but she couldn't. She was 64, and suddenly had five other mouths to feed. She had raised Gabrielle, her twelve-year-old granddaughter, since she was a baby. Her daughter brought her over late one night and asked Bessie to take care of her for a couple days, then she just disappeared. Bessie hasn't heard from her since.

Eleven-year-old Katrina was a neighborhood stray. Three years ago she started coming over every day to play with Gabrielle. Bessie would ask her when she had to be home for dinner, and Katrina would shrug her shoulders and say they didn't have dinner at her house. Bessie would call her mother to see if it would be OK for her to feed her. Most of the time, no one answered the phone.

Katrina first started eating meals at Bessie's, then she started spending the night. Bessie bought her a toothbrush, pajamas, then underwear and some clothes that she kept for her at the house, and it just evolved from there. Katrina's mother had her own issues, and she seemed relieved to not have the burden of raising a daughter.

Then, last September, Bessie's other daughter checked herself into rehab and dropped off her three kids. There was eight-year-old Ellie, thirteen- year-old Leslie, then there was Michael. He had just turned fifteen, was big for his age, and getting to be a handful. Soon after they arrived, he grew sullen and distant. Bessie wasn't happy with some of the company he was keeping. They were some rough kids who hung out at the brown house on the corner.

She did the best she could, but she was growing weary. Bessie was the last stop for those kids and she wasn't going to abandon them. She worried about them constantly and it was taking a toll on her.

Bessie also worried about Leonard. She guessed he had to be past seventy, and he had no one to look after him. He lived in a one room efficiency on the second floor of an apartment building where everyone shared the same bathroom down the hall. He had a hot plate, a small TV, a single fold up bed, and little else. He didn't need much else, he said. The more stuff he owned, he once told Bessie, the more he'd just have to take care of.

Early in December, he mentioned to Bessie that he hadn't been sleeping too well. He also hadn't had much of an appetite. He'd lost enough weight that his snowman suit was hanging loose on him. He started stuffing it with a few pillows, which wasn't so bad as it made it a bit warmer. Being a mime was also growing more challenging. His muscles cramped and he found it more difficult to hold a pose. He was tired most of the time. Walking up the stairs to his apartment left him out of breath. Bessie wondered how much longer he could keep it up.

It was the day before the day before Christmas. Leonard arrived at 1:00 as usual, but the weather was threatening. The temperature plummeted, the wind picked up, and the sky grew dark. A fine sleet started to fall and it continued throughout the afternoon. By 3:30 the parking lot was a sheet of ice. Only the very brave or the not so smart ventured out on a day like this. Few people were coming into the store. Around 4:30, Leonard checked his kettle and counted $51 – two twenties, a ten, a dollar bill, and some change. The two $20 bills came from a man in a suit, driving a big black SUV. He pulled into the parking lot shortly after 1:00, rolled down his window, dropped the two bills in the kettle, and drove away.

Leonard was not feeling well. He was cold and wet, and felt a fever coming on. The roads were bad, and as evening drew near, he figured that few, if any, would be coming to the store. He decided to pack it in, skip the shopping and deliveries, and just head home. No one would blame him. Besides, tomorrow was Christmas Eve, and he'd make it up then.

He picked up his kettle and turned to begin the three-block walk towards home when he heard someone coming up behind him quite fast. He didn't have time to turn to see who it was. He heard the footsteps coming, then whoever it was brushed by him, snatched the kettle out of his hands, and ran. It looked like a big kid. He grabbed the few bills that were inside and then threw the kettle over his shoulder and kept on going. The bucket hit the frozen parking lot and loose change went everywhere.

Leonard couldn't catch a glimpse of the boy's face. He took two steps to give chase and then thought better of it. With the second step, his heart just grabbed him. It felt like someone drove a dagger deep into his chest. He put his hand to his heart and bent over with pain. He paused for a second to gather himself.

After a minute or two, the pain lessened enough for him to retrieve the kettle and scoop up a couple quarters. He let the rest of the coins go when the pain returned. He backed up a step to the curb, leaned back against the mailbox, and slid down on his bottom, with the kettle resting in his lap.

"Just rest a second and catch my breath," Leonard thought. Thankfully, it had been a slow day and the kid didn't get off with much. Leonard would more than make it for up tomorrow. It wasn't worth the hassle of chasing him down. Let him go. Just rest here for a few minutes, then he'd head home and go to bed.

He felt so heavy in the chest, like a circus elephant was sitting on him, and he was having a hard time getting a deep breath. His left shoulder and arm were numb, but the stabbing pain in his chest seemed to be subsiding. "Just give me another minute," he thought to himself. "I'll be all right."

There wasn't a car in the parking lot. Not a soul was around. It was dusk, and no one was on the road either. Leonard sat there against the mailbox. Just a couple more minutes and he'd head home. He leaned back, tilted his head up and closed his eyes. He thought about the kid. Who was he? And where were his parents? Why would he do something like that at Christmas? He prayed for the boy, whoever he was. Maybe his family was desperate and he was just trying to provide for them. Leonard wanted to think the best of people.

He rested there for a while. By the mailbox, he was at least out of the freezing rain. His mind wandered. He thought about Jeanette, about their years together at the circus. He could picture her long brown hair and sweet smile. She was so beautiful. He remembered the way she would look into his eyes so tenderly when she wanted to get his attention, how she would gently brush his cheek and arrange his hair away from his eyes with her soft hands. He remembered how she felt when they snuggled on the couch to watch TV. Oh, how he missed her.

He thought about lots of things. He thought about his time in Viet Nam. He remembered his buddies who didn't make it home. He thought about his mother, about his family back in Kentucky and Christmases past. He thought about the Lord.

Sitting on an icy curb, with the wind stinging his face, Leonard felt strangely warmed by a surge of gratitude.

He'd get up in a few seconds and head home. He didn't feel as cold and the pain seemed to be going away. He'd be O.K. Rest here another moment and he'd be on

his way. Get home and into some dry clothes. A soft warm
bed was waiting. "Just a minute more . . ."

By mid-morning the following day, the rain had
stopped and the sun started to break through the clouds.
The temperature had risen and the ice was melting. The
parking lot filled up quickly with shoppers. It was
Christmas Eve.

Frosty was sitting against the mailbox. His eyes were
open and a relaxed smile lined his face. People dropped
dollar bills and change in the kettle as they walked by.
One older woman pulling a little boy by the hand stopped
a few feet from Frosty and studied him. "It's amazing!" she
said, as she waved her hand in front of Frosty's face. "How
does he do it? It's as if he isn't breathing!" Then she
grabbed the boy, turned, and went inside.

Christmas sometimes does that to people. It puts us all
in a rush and we miss things.

Around 11:00, someone realized that something
wasn't right. A woman went into the store, found Mr.
Pringle, and told him, "I think something's wrong with
Frosty." Mr. Pringle was surprised to hear that Frosty was
there this early in the day. "He doesn't usually arrive until
1:00 or so." He felt terrible. He was so busy he hadn't
even checked the front of the store to see him there.

Mr. Pringle hurried outside. A small crowd of people huddled around Frosty. A woman, a nurse it turned out, was on her knees on the sidewalk, checking his pulse. Someone had called 911. An ambulance soon arrived, and then a police car. They loaded Frosty on to a gurney and took him away.

Mr. Pringle stood at attention as the van pulled out of the parking lot. Its lights were running, but there was no need for a siren. He watched it disappear down the road when a policeman approached and asked a couple questions. A second officer reached into the squad car and grabbed the kettle out of the back seat. He walked up and handed it to Mr. Pringle. It was filled to the brim with money.

"What do you want me to do with this?" he asked.

The officers shrugged their shoulders. "We don't know. You knew him as well as anyone. You'd know what he would have done with it." And with that, both of them got into their car and drove away.

Mr. Pringle looked down at the kettle in his hands. It was heavy and full. As he stood there, people walked past and stuffed the thing even more. He turned and went inside, made his way through the crowd of shoppers to his office and closed the door. He set the kettle on his desk. From the size of the pile and the number of bills, he guessed there might be close to $2,000 in there.

He didn't have time to count it. There was work that had to be done around the store.

Early in the afternoon, when he had a break, he grabbed a box of gallon zip lock bags, returned to his office, and started stuffing the bags with the money from the kettle. He filled seven bags in all, put them in a white canvas shopping bag, then went back to work.

With what happened to Frosty, the crowds, and the holiday rush, the day had flown by. Mr. Pringle stopped by his office to check his e-mail when he noticed the clock. It was getting close to 4:30.

Just then there was a knock on the door. It was Bessie. Her eyes were filled with tears. She cried, "Oh, Mr. Pringle! Isn't it so sad about Frosty! I wish I would have checked on him earlier. They said he had been gone for several hours."

Mr. Pringle couldn't think of anything to say. He just sighed, pressed his lips together, looked at Bessie and gave a faint smile. Frosty was one of the kindest men they had ever known. What would Pringle's be without him?

Bessie paused and then continued. "Mr. Pringle, do you mind if I go home early? I don't know that I'm much good to you anymore today, and besides, we talked about this last week, that I could go home early Christmas Eve to be with my kids. I promised to take them to the Christmas Eve service at church."

Mr. Pringle walked over to Bessie and gave her a hug. "Of course you can, Bess. You go right ahead. We'll cover things here." Then he walked over to his desk and grabbed the white shopping bag with the seven zip lock bags, turned, and handed them to her.

The bag was heavy. "What am I to do with these?" she asked with a bit of shock in her voice.

"You knew him better than anyone," Mr. Pringle said. "You'd know exactly what he would have done with that money. Besides, you've had a lot on your plate lately. I imagine you could put some of this to good use yourself. Merry Christmas Bessie."

She stood there speechless. Mr. Pringle then remembered that she didn't have a car. "Here, I'll help you with these, let me take care of a few last minute things, and I'll take you home."

After he did what he had to do, and gave some instructions to his assistant, Mr. Pringle grabbed the money, called Bessie, and led her out to his car. He drove the five blocks to her two-bedroom duplex and helped her carry the bags and her other things inside. He set the bags on the kitchen table, wished them all a Merry Christmas, and headed out the door.

The kids came to the kitchen to see Bessie standing over the table. She dumped the cloth bag out to reveal seven gallon-ziplock bags full of money.

The children's jaws dropped. "Whose is that, Grandma?"

"I'm guessing it's ours."

"How much is it?

"I don't know."

"What are we going to do with it?"

"I don't know that either."

She had them all sit down, and she told the children about Frosty, about how kind he was and about all the good that he did, and how he died suddenly and how no one knew it until the middle of day. She dabbed at her tears with a dish towel as she told them. The kids listened quietly.

Bessie finished her story, then gathered herself. "Well, whatever we do with it, I want to use it in a way that would honor Frosty, use it the way he would have wanted." She stood up and gathered what little energy she could muster. "But we'll have to figure that out later. We have to get to the Christmas Eve service. C'mon, brush your teeth, get ready and get your coats on. We're leaving in twenty minutes."

She turned and went to her room to change into her Sunday dress. When she was ready, she came back out to the kitchen and saw Michael still sitting at the table. His head was resting on folded arms. He was meditating on the bags of money.

"Sugar, are you coming?"

He glanced at her briefly, then back to the bags. "No, you go ahead, Grandma. Christmas Eve church is for kids. I think I'll just stay here."

Bessie worried about him, and she worried about all that money sitting there, but she didn't have the energy to fight with him, not on Christmas Eve. "Alright girls, let's go." They headed out the door and began the four-block walk in the other direction to the church.

Michael heard the door slam shut, then turned his thoughts back to the bags of money.

No one had counted it yet. No one would know if some of it was missing. His heart pounded inside his chest. His head pounded too - in a barrage of conflicting thoughts that were jousting with each other. Guilt and justification, duty then desire fought for the upper hand.

What could he do?

What should he do?

Then, in a moment, like the sudden parting of storm clouds, Michael knew what he had to do. It became as clear as day what he had to do, and he had a sudden rush of resolve to do it.

He pushed his chair away from the table, stood, and made his way to his bedroom, which wasn't anything more than a cot and a small dresser down at the end of the hall. He pulled open the bottom drawer, reached under a t-shirt and found $51 – two $20's, a $10, and a $1. He then opened the top drawer and pulled out $27 that he had earned doing chores and cutting his neighbor's lawn.

Michael checked the time. It was 6:15. The store closed in forty-five minutes. He could make it if he hurried. He gathered the money from his drawer, grabbed his coat and ran to Pringle's department store. Upon arriving, he walked down each aisle and loaded his cart with cloth work gloves and some blankets, then he went back to the lunch counter for some sandwiches and hot coffee. He paid for the stuff, then wheeled the cart out the door, around the back, through the employee parking lot, through a hole in the back fence, across the railroad track, and into the woods where the homeless community lived.

He delivered the gifts. They thanked him but then asked, "Who are you?" They had already heard about Frosty. News travels fast on the street. "I guess I'm his substitute," Michael said, and then he left and went back the way he came.

He checked his smart phone. It was 7:40. If he hurried, he could get to the church before the service ended. He returned the cart to the store and then ran nearly a mile to the church. He walked in just as the last carol was being sung. He made his way down to the front and pulled in next to his grandma. He surprised her, but she smiled at him and shared her candle and her hymnal.

He got in on the final two verses:

> *How silently, how silently*
> *The wondrous gift is given!*
> *So God imparts to human hearts*
> *The blessings of His heaven.*
> *No ear may hear His coming,*
> *But in this world of sin,*
> *Where meek souls will receive him still,*
> *The dear Christ enters in.*

> *O little child of Bethlehem*
> *Descend on us we pray.*
> *Cast out our sin and enter in*
> *Be born in us today.*

We hear the Christmas angels
The great glad tidings tell.
O come to us, abide with us
Our Lord, Immanuel

As the people sang, the overhead lights were dimmed and the church filled with candlelight. Standing and singing next to his grandma, Michael felt different. She looked different to him.

The whole world somehow seemed different. He couldn't describe it. It was something beyond words that he would keep to himself. He just felt new. He felt clean. He felt a feeling that he thought might be what it feels like to be a man. He felt responsible. He felt confident. He could be the one man in a house full of women who needed him.

————————————————

There's a postscript to the story. After the holidays, Michael was seen perusing thrift shops, looking for black boots and scarves and hats. He was also spotted at the library, checking out books on how to be a mime.

————————————————

It's no mystery how a human heart can grow hard. It's just a matter of time, and then it happens. Life's constant battery of wounds and sorrows, fears and desires takes its toll, and the heart grows hard and resistant, smothered by layers of defenses and lies. It is not a mystery at all. It happens, to some extent, to us all.

It is a great mystery, however, how, in an instant, a hardened heart can grow soft. In just a moment, in a flash of insight, inspiration, conviction, and clarity, a hardened heart can grow soft again.

This happens too. It happened for Michael. It can happen for me. It can happen for you, too. It's entirely possible - because changing hardened hearts into something pliable that He can use for His glory is what God does. It is the business that He has been up to from the beginning.

It is why He came.

Made in the USA
Columbia, SC
27 September 2020